The
END
ZONE

L.J. SHEN

The End Zone
Cover Designer: Letitia Hasser, RBA Designs
Interior Formatting: Stacey Blake, Champagne Book Design

"Love looks not with the eyes, but with the mind,
And therefore is winged Cupid painted blind."
**—William Shakespeare, A Midsummer Night's
Dream**

The END ZONE

Jolie Louis is a smart girl.

She knows that her best friend, Gabe Poirier, is a bad idea.

He's a walking, talking cliché. The Adonis quarterback with the bulging biceps and harem of fangirls trailing behind him on campus like a stench you can't get rid of.

Sadly, that's also the reason she can't stay away from him. Well, that and the fact that they're roommates.

Jolie is already straddling the line between friendship and more when Sage comes to her with an offer she cannot refuse: be his fake girlfriend and live for free for the rest of the semester.

She tells herself that she can handle it.

He's just the boy she saved ten years ago, right?

Wrong. So very wrong.

He is a man now, and she is his captive

Heart, body, and soul…

Prologue

Ten years ago.

O n the eighth night, she decided to talk to
him.

Eight nights since the Poiriers had
waltzed into her life, occupying the house next door.

Eight nights in which the screaming, yelling,
and crying of Mrs. Poirier and the roars of her husband pierced Jolie's ears, trickled into her soul, and
left her trembling under the quilt her grandmama
had made for her.

Eight nights in which their kid—about her age,
ten or eleven—stumbled to their squeaky porch, his
dirty blond hair sticking out in every direction and
his chest heaving with uneven breaths.

Cheeks stained pink.

Mouth curled in a dark scowl.

Eyes blazing hot, red rage she could see even in

the pitch-black of the night.

Eight nights that he'd been climbing the oak tree which divided the land between the Poiriers' and her house. He sat there, hidden by branches and leaves. Sometimes he howled to the moon like a lonely wolf. Most times, he cried as silently as humanly possible.

Seven sleepless nights in which *she* tossed and turned and mourned for the nameless boy and his mama, before she broke down and decided to approach him. Even if he'd yell at her. Even if he'd laugh at her. Even if he'd show her no mercy like his daddy had taught him.

The girl pushed her window up with a groan, dragged an old case of books across the carpeted floor, hopped on it, and slipped through the open crack, pouring from the safety of her bedroom to the untamed, uncut meadow. The rain pounded hard on her face, the wind swooshing in her ears. It was humid, hot, muggy, and sticky. Her white cotton pajama dress clung to her skin, rain dripping from its hem to her feet. The grass was slippery, and mud coated her toes. The boy was trudging to the tree determinedly. She cautiously ambled in the same direction.

He slowed when he saw her, so she picked up the pace. Later in life, she'd learn that this was their special tango. One pulls, the other pushes. One wants, the other gives. One loves, the other hurts.

"What are you doing here?" he yelled through the rain. It was impossible to answer him. Her heart was in her throat, pounding *boom, boom, boom* like a caged animal craving freedom.

Step, another step, then another. She wondered if that's how it felt to be alive. Really alive. Not just living. Wet, uncomfortable, and shivering in the midst of a hot summer storm. Up close, he looked even angrier, his eyes a terrifying hue of midnight blue and ire.

They stopped about six feet from each other, right next to the tree. He was slightly taller, slightly wider, face slightly tenser, and a lot warier than she expected.

"Well?" he repeated, brooding. *He is far too young to brood*, she remembered thinking. And it worried her, despite all reason (their brief history). "Why the hell are you here?"

"I'm sorry," she said, swallowing the pain she carried for him. Like stars in her pocket—it was huge, and she couldn't begin to understand how she'd harbored it for eight nights. He needed help, and she wanted to give it to him.

They'd start school in a couple of weeks—fifth grade—and he'd be the new kid. She decided right then and there that she was going to be his ally. She'd be his friend, whether he liked it or not.

"You're sorry?" He snorted out a bitter laugh, shaking his head. Raindrops ran from the tip of his straight nose, his full lips flattening in an angry line. "Well, don't be. I'm perfectly fine."

"You don't look fine," she insisted.

"Well, I am."

"I'm here for you." She hugged her midsection, embarrassed. Her grandmama used to say that honesty made you vulnerable, but that there was nothing stronger than the truth.

"Whatever you need, I'm here for you. I'm Jolie, by the way." She stretched her hand between them. He stared at it silently, contemplating, like she offered him much more than a handshake. And maybe she did. The whole thing felt bizarre. Grown-up. The oak tree beside them looked like a living thing, watching as they made this unlikely pact.

"Sage," he said, his palm connecting with hers.

She squeezed hard; he inhaled harder. He jerked her to his body, buried his head in the crook of her shoulder, and shook with tears she couldn't see.

They hugged in the rain, just like in the movies.

They hugged long, and tight, and desperately, his skin soaking into hers like a kiss.

The girl thought to herself, *this is how beautiful love stories begin.* She pressed her ear against his thrumming pulse. His body was warm, but his muscles were rigid like ice.

The girl closed her eyes and the storm disappeared. Not because it had stopped, but because beside him, she felt fearless.

And on the eighth night, the girl gave the boy more than friendship and a hug, without even meaning to—and definitely without agreeing to.

On the eighth night, the girl gave the boy her heart.

He took it silently, never offering his back.

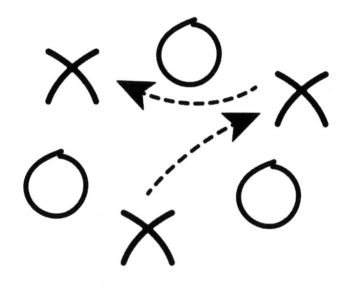

Chapter
ONE

Jolie

"Yo, JoJo. Your ass is on wingman duty tonight." A steaming Starbucks mug slides across the shiny chrome desk he bought for me last Christmas. I lift my head, skeptically examining him through my hazel eyes.

Sage Poirier. My best friend. Louisiana's finest college quarterback. The man who put the 'ho' in manwhore. My forever crush. The list goes on, but I'm sure you get the point. I rearrange the golden neckline of my sensible powder blue blouse, tossing my strawberry blonde tresses (heavy on the strawberry) across my shoulder.

"I have an English lit exam tomorrow." I yawn, my hand already hovering over the keyboard of my MacBook. The bribe—pumpkin spice latte with marshmallows, not technically on the menu, but the barista would throw in her own kidney to get Sage to smile at her—is appreciated, albeit pointless. With the amount of homework I have, I'm not going to budge from my seat tonight. Sage grabs the chair opposite to me and plops backwards on a heavy sigh, his arms bracing its back. He is wearing his black New Orleans Saints cap backwards, his Wayfarers hanging under the brim of his hat from behind. It's the indisputable, international I'm-a-douchebag badge, and it occurs to me, for the hundredth time since we moved in together freshman year of college, that if I hadn't known him since age ten, I would probably find him as sexually attractive as a gassy rat.

"You're no fun." He leans forward and flicks his thumb and finger on the tip of my nose. His mischievous, dimpled smile widens when I swat his hand away.

"I have grades to keep," I retort.

"So do I."

I snort a laugh on an eye roll. "You're one of the most sought-after quarterbacks in Louisiana. Going pro next year. At this point, you can flake your way to being a brain surgeon if you'd like. Every professor in this college would kiss the earth you walk upon if they didn't fear you'd file a restraining order against them."

Sadly, it isn't even an exaggeration. Don't get me wrong—I'm thrilled for my best friend. He deserves everything he's achieved, which is *a lot*. At twenty-one, he has his own shiny, burgundy truck, a brand new apartment he rents all by himself (I pay the bills in exchange for my room), and three NFL teams courting him like he is a damsel in a Disney movie. Despite all his success, he's never once been uppity or conceited to me about it. Instead, he gives me access to his new place, new truck, and new life. He is still the good Southern mama's boy who takes off his hat whenever he visits the small farm we lived on. The only downside to being Sage's best friend is, well…

"Question is—do *you* want to kiss the ground I walk on, or better yet, *me*?" His elbows are on the desk now, his head cocked to the side attentively. "Because, Jolie, baby, you're the only person I'm looking to impress. Ideally between the sheets." He winks.

Insert an emoji of moi gagging uncontrollably at his tackiness.

This is not the first time Sage has made a move on me, and I bet it won't be the last time I shut him down.

A month ago, Sage and I accidentally bumped into each other in the hallway while I was butt naked after a shower (forgot the towel in my room). He was on his way to pee, sporting impressive morning wood through his gray boxers. I was looking down, head hanging in shame as I hurried to my room. He was looking down, rearranging his junk. That's how we ended up colliding, limbs tangling together, with me tumbling down and him reaching for my ass to make sure I didn't fall. What a gentleman, right?

From that point forward, Sage has been adamant that we need to hook up. Emphasis on the word 'need' and not 'should'.

And, Lord, forgive me. If he were any other guy, I'd be all over him like a rash after a torrid Vegas vacation. The man looks like the love child of Matthew Noszka and James Dean. The fact that he is six feet four inches of tight abs and only five percent body fat does not—I repeat, does not—make it easier for me to constantly reject him. But you know what makes it really easy for me to say no? The notion that Sage, whom I grew up with and know better than anyone else, is going to break my heart into a trillion pieces, smash it to dust, then skip over all the leftovers on his way to the next pink sheet-covered bed.

Because. My. Best. Friend. Is. A. Whore!

I love him, but he is a manwhore who can't keep his dick in his pants for longer than twenty-four hours. I'm pretty sure this fact could be backed up scientifically, if someone put effort into researching the subject. Anyway, I'm too attached to Sage—and to my heart—to mess with either of them so recklessly.

"It's a no from me," I say in an exaggerated English accent, folding my arms and feigning boredom, doing my best Simon Cowell impression. We've been bingeing on the British version of *X Factor* lately and Sage makes me do an impression of the British judge every commercial break. If I refuse, he tackles me to the floor and tickles the shit out of me. I thrash and try to worm my way out from between his steel arms, only to be pinned tightly onto the floor, his hard body over mine. He is so aggressive and dedicated, ninety percent of the time I cave simply because I'm too scared I'll accidentally come or fart (hey, just keeping it real).

"I'll turn it into a 'yes' before the end of the semester." He stands up, curling his fists as he stretches and yawns. His black shirt rides up and the prominent V leading to his crotch is on full display. In a last-ditch effort to save my panties, I avert my gaze, my eyes hard on the MacBook screen, and furrow my brows as the words in my lit essay slip from my vision. I decided to major in English lit because I'm good with words, but whenever he's around, I'm nothing but a blubbery mess. He continues, "No girl has ever said no to me yet, and I'll be damned if the one who does is the chick I care about the most."

"But that's exactly why I'm saying no," I snap, my head shooting up from the essay, annoyed he'd joke about our friendship.

"Why?"

Why? "Why?" I look up, huffing. Yep, I'm actually huffing. And huffers are my pet peeve, but boy, does Sage make me want to huff lately. "Do you really want to throw away ten years of friendship for a quick lay?"

He smirks. "First of all, it's not going to be quick. I know what I'm doing in the sack. We're talking a minimum of twenty-five minutes, lady, and I'm being humble here, because I might be a little on the excited side when I finally get you in my bed." He cups his groin and winks, and I would roll my eyes if it weren't for the fact that his room is down the hall, and the thin walls confirm his statement. All the girls he brings home (roughly twenty percent of the US female population) *do* moan and scream for an average of forty minutes. "And second of all, I will not be ruining anything. You have one-night stands. I have one-night stands. We can have them together and still keep our friendship intact. We're not fucking twelve, dude."

I guess I can kill this conversation by pointing out that (A) twelve-year-olds don't usually have sexual intercourse, and (B) I'm not a dude. But there's something else I need to make clear.

"I don't engage in one-night stands." I pick up a pen and choke it to death to keep myself from punching Sage's gorgeous, cocky face. I know my fist is going to be hurt more than his nose. The guy is seemingly built of steel, bronze, and copper.

"*Of* course you do. What about that Brandon dude?"

"*That* Brandon dude was my boyfriend for seven months," I deadpan. Funny he should mention it, since Brandon and I broke up last year because he was adamant that there was something going on between Sage and me. Which was insane, inaccurate, and incredibly annoying. But what was even more disheartening was the fact that Sage did everything he could to nurture this false assumption by constantly touching and calling me whenever I hung out with Brandon like he was trying to sabotage our relationship. Sage was only a few weeks short of pissing on my leg to claim his ownership, which was kind of rich, considering how Sage's dick has been passed around like community property. I'm surprised he's not partly funded by the government.

"That douche was never your boyfriend, JoJo."

"Sorry to disappoint, but he really was."

"Well, he didn't know that. I still want to kick that guy's ass."

"What? Why?"

"Because—*sorry to disappoint,*" he mimics my

tone, and pretty accurately, too (the bastard), "but he was banging a Kappa Alpha Slutta whatever chick named Nadia. I saw them hanging out at parties at least twice, but I kind of thought you'd never actually seriously dated the dickbag, yeah?" He runs his huge palm over his sandy blond hair and messes it to tousled perfection. I swallow, feeling my nostrils flare. Goddamn Brandon. "So I never thought I should mention it to you. You know I always got your back."

I smile tightly, stand up, and walk to the kitchen with Sage following behind me. I want him gone, so I can cry myself to sleep, or call my bestie, Chelsea, to talk so much shit about Brandon his ears catch on fire and burn down his whole apartment block. I feel played, and stupid, and about as desirable as a bowl of stale broccoli even though it's been months.

"Come with me," Sage coaxes again, his husky voice seeping into my body and melting my lady parts into warm goo. What's wrong with me? This is my best friend we're talking about. Countless times I watched him go home with other girls, puking in national parks, and experiencing meltdowns. Crying happily when his parents got divorced, weeping sadly when his father died of liver failure after years of alcohol abuse, and roaring triumphantly when he got a full scholarship for college.

"I have an exam, remember?" I open the fridge

and take out a carton of OJ. I slam the door and when I turn around, he is caging me in, bracing the counter from each side of my waist, his mouth so close to mine I can see the dimple in the center of his full lower lip. He stares me down predatorily.

My heart is in my throat.

My soul is most probably in my eyes.

And I am scared. Completely, utterly, and desperately frightened of what he can do to me if I let my guard down. If I let him.

"Wasn't talking about the party, Jo. Let's go to my room. Forget about Brandon. About people. About all the bullshit. I want to make you feel good."

"Sage," I hiss, narrowing my eyes. "Please don't make this an issue. I'd hate to move to another apartment, but I will, if that's what it takes to save our friendship."

And my heart.

He throws his head back and shakes it, staring at the ceiling, exasperated. Then he pushes off the counter and I'm left to stand here, watching his tight ass walking toward the hallway. What's with this dude? Did he actually not know I had lady bits before he saw me naked? I refuse to sacrifice our friendship because he suddenly sees me as a convenient fuck. He's been acting so strange lately.

I watch his back, knowing the knot in my stomach—the one I'd formed when I was ten and he moved next door—is going to tighten. As if on cue, it does. Blinking, I pour myself a glass of orange juice, spilling some on the countertop, knowing the rest of my night is a bust.

Twenty minutes later, he walks through the door clad in a navy varsity jacket, dark distressed jeans, and his I-just-fucked perfect hair, looking like the perfect sin.

Forty minutes later, Chelsea appears at my door armed with Halo Top ice cream. (I liked Brandon, but not enough to waste my Pilates body on real ice cream because of him.)

An hour later, I get a stream of text messages.

Sage: Dedication doesn't have an off-season. Get ready for me, JoJo. Because I'm coming for you. And guess what? You'll COME for me, too.

Sage: Please told me you got the sexual innuendo.

Sage: *tell. Not told. Don't give me shit. I'm not drunk.

Sage: Also, we're out of milk, but don't worry, I'll buy some on the way home. Notice how I don't didn't use any sexual innuendo even though it's white and sticky…

10

Chapter
TWO

Sage

"Please tell me you didn't forget to ask her this time."

Mark's elbow is propped against the kitchen island I'm leaning on. The party is a bust. Even though it's at a big-ass mansion on the outskirts of Baton Rouge, the vibe is just...*off*. Every fucker in my year seems to be here and I don't know half of these people who talk to me, but everyone knows *me*. This chains me into a string of endless, meaningless, mundane conversations about grades and football, two things I shouldn't be thinking about during my time off.

Mark snaps his fingers in front of my eyes and I blink, realizing that he's been doing it for some time now. He is the tall, dark, handsome, nice-enough-not-to-fuck-his-secretary-in-twenty-years type. Congressman daddy. English teacher mommy. Three sisters. Perfect reputation. White picket fence and two dogs with adorably stupid names. Wholesome and nice. He is the exact opposite of *me*.

I chew on the red Solo cup that I'm holding and zone out again, letting the half-naked bodies and the heaps of alcohol melt together in my vision.

"Asked who what?" I buy time.

"Your hot roommate. Did you ask her if she's into me?" Again, I find myself wanting to punch my own balls for downplaying my relationship with Jolie. This is all my doing, and the reason I don't tell people how close we are is because I don't want any cock-blocking scenarios to get in my way of a good pussy. Well, this month it backfired in my face. Not only did I experience a life-changing moment with another girl, which pretty much served as a wake-up call to who I *really* need to be with, but now I have to deal with my smitten teammate, too.

Ever since Mark Tensely struck up a thirty-minute-long conversation with Jolie when he swung by to pick up some football gear the other day (specifically the day before I ran into her naked in the hall-way—*insert fucking fist-bite*) he's been eyeing my best friend and begging for me to hook him up with her number.

Yeah. No.

12

Perhaps the worst part is that Mark is smart, good-looking, rich, and is actively seeking a steady girlfriend. Unlike Barf-worthy Brandon, he's actually genuine. The whole package. Me? The only thing I have to offer *is* my package. I'm swimming in small endorsement deals and have a scholarship, but I'm so far from well off, I can barely fucking spell the term. Plus, Jolie knows about my antics. She constantly tells me that STD stands for Sage the Douche. We joke about it, like it doesn't worry her and it doesn't insult me. But the truth is, my string of one-night stands have all ended in disaster recently. Though, even before that, I was starting to get bored with the constant hopping from one strange bed to the other.

Look, I know I'm a hypocritical bastard. I fuck around, but the minute my roommate gets a suitor, I go all Jason Momoa on his ass. But I can't control it, can I? And if it makes things slightly better, I haven't porked anyone since Mark made that comment about JoJo. Between throwing him off, dealing with my latest disastrous fling, and jerking off to memories of Jolie's naked body, sex with strangers is the last thing on my mind.

Thing is, I can't really relationship-block Mark right now. What the fuck would I say to him? "Hey, listen, man, there's nothing going on between Jolie and me, but I still don't want her to date you?" Even

I know it's a solid ten on the Douche-O-Meter. It would be much easier to just say, "Look, bro, I'm tapping that. Why don't you go ahead and move along to someone less attractive and, I don't know, less *Jolie*?"

"Jolie! I've been asking you to ask her about me for weeks. Forget it." Mark waves me off, grabbing a beer bottle from the fridge. There's a keg right. Freaking. Here. But I guess he's too rich for Solo cups. "I'll just ask her out. I see her around campus every Monday at three."

Over my dead body, bro.

"Get some chill, yeah? I got a lot on my plate this month. I'll ask her as soon as I get home." I clutch his shoulder and offer him the most casual smile in my arsenal. Inside, there's a green angry monster wreaking havoc in my body. If Mark takes Jolie on a date, it wouldn't be the first time she went out with someone else. JoJo had two serious boyfriends in high school and dated a string of douches ever since we started college. But they all seemed so temporary. Her mind was always elsewhere. School. Family. Even the Pilates classes that gave her that bangin' body. But this is all going to change at the end of May when we graduate. I know my best friend. Know her well.

She'll want to settle down.

Find a nice teaching job.

Get married. Have babies. Mark's babies. No way is she having Mark's babies. That fucker doesn't drink keg beer and knows how to tie a tie without looking in the mirror. He's not the type to run in the mud and rain for her. To climb on trees with her. To sit on the sidelines at school and talk shit about people in codes only she and he know.

I'm that person. I'm *her* person.

"I'll deal with it tonight," I stress again.

"Yeah, okay, man," Mark mumbles, pupils dilating, and that's when I realize that I'm squeezing his shoulder super fucking hard. He shakes me off, taking a step back and bumping into two girls who are yelling the latest gossip into each other's ears over the sound of "Fetish" by Selena Gomez. They both shoot him a pissed look that softens when they notice me. "I'll text you tomorrow." Mark points at me. Is this a fucking threat? I don't owe him shit. Better to get it out of the way, though, than have him approaching her on his own.

"Sure." I shrug, raising my cup in the air and backing toward the landing. "See you Monday at practice."

You know shit is going downhill when you find yourself listening to a pop princess and there's no blowie to stop you from leaving. I turn around and a girl from computer science slams into my body purposely. She does the whole laughing nervously and pretending to be embarrassed charade—*sweetheart, I've seen this show a thousand times*—and introduces herself. I can take her home. Hell, I can even take her upstairs. A month ago, I would have. But tonight, all I can think about is that Jolie is hella bummed about what I told her about Brandon, and I'm bummed about that goddamn tool, Mark.

"I'm Stephanie," she yells into my ear.

"And I'm not interested," I yell back.

The mask of her syrupy smile falls to the floor, almost with a thud, and her eyes narrow before she sulks and leaves. I dig out my phone and send Jolie a string of semi-coherent text messages. Then I come up with a plan to eliminate Mark Tensely from the picture.

By the time I drive back home, stone-cold sober, making a stop at a gas station to get some milk, my plan is bulletproof.

Jolie is not dating anyone.

Jolie stays with me.

Chapter
THREE

Jolie

"We need to talk."

Reluctantly, I crack one eye open, while still rolled between my white cotton sheets, the TV still playing the same channel I fell asleep to the night before. After Chelsea left, I watched *When Harry Met Sally*. Then I opened a bottle of wine, downed three glasses, and waited for the alcohol to run through my bloodstream before I willed myself to answer my male BFF's texts.

Me: Do you think Brandon cheated on me because I'm a prude?

Me: Maybe it's because I went to see my family

every other weekend when he wanted to hang out. Although, screw him, right? So I like spending time with my grandmama and parents. Ain't no shame in that.

Me: And yes to you bringing milk. I will need something to help the hangover tomorrow morning.

Me: And no to you and me sleeping together. I already told you, Sage. I care too much about you to lose you for a fling. Even if the feeling is obviously not mutual...

My bed dips under the weight of my quarterback guy friend and I bury my face into my pillow, inhaling the vanilla, lilac, and lavender of my body creams and shampoo. His warm hand sneaks under the covers, cupping one of my feet and tugging me away from the pillow and toward him. With my ankle on his lap, he massages my foot. And I should really get a gold medal, or maybe a simple acknowledgement, for not spreading my legs for him right here and now and giving him exactly what he has been begging for.

Because. Sage. Poirier. Is. A. God!

That's why he's a manwhore in the first place. There is no denying his masculine appeal, raw beauty, dirty mouth, and cocky confidence.

"What do we need to talk about?" I murmur into my arm, which I've thrown over my face to block the sun seeping through the thin curtains of my window. He elevates my foot and kisses just below my kneecap. Shivers run down my spine, racing down to my tummy and making it roll with delicious anticipation.

"I need a fake girlfriend," he announces, his voice grave.

"Then go get one. Literally, you can step out of the building and every single woman with a pulse and no ring on her ring finger would gladly fill out an application," I say, hyper-aware to my morning breath. He plucks my arm from my face and throws it on the bed, leaning into me so we are nose-to-nose.

Great. Just great. Now he can smell my dead hyena breath.

"I'm serious," comes his dark whisper, and he no longer sounds like my Sage. I mean, Sage. He is not mine. I know that. Duh.

"So am I. Why do you need a fake girlfriend?" I speak into my cupped hand, my eyebrows crinkling.

"Want the truth?"

"No, please lie to me. But make it a spectacular lie. Something with unicorns." I widen my blurry eyes, and he chuckles, grabbing one of the pillows I kicked in my sleep and throwing it in my face.

"Rascal," he says.

"Wifebeater," I groan. He stands still, stares at me. *What?* It was a figure of speech. I didn't mean it like I was literally his wife.

"I can't tell you why, but I can tell you that you're the only girl for the job. I have a Christmas fund-raising thing happening in New York next month and I need someone on my arm. You're the only girl, other than my mama, I'd like to take with me. The only one I trust not to let me down. And my mama can't get time off work, so that leaves me with you. Say yes."

I swallow, not really sure how this is different from all the other times I accompanied Sage to his football events. There's something desperate and utterly determined in the way he looks at me. Like there are so many words on the tip of his tongue that he's biting down, afraid to use.

"I don't need to be your fake girlfriend for that."

"You do. It's important. Everyone at school needs to know that we're a thing."

"But why?"

"I'd tell you, but then I'd have to kill you. Now, I'm pretty sure I'd be a top in jail, not a bottom, but still—not really into dudes. So, yes?"

Ugh with this man. "Ugh with you. What do *I* get out of this?"

Before you throw rotten tomatoes at me (under-standable), accompanied by a collective 'boo' (rea-sonable)—let me explain why I ask: there's definitely something Sage is gaining from this, no doubt at all, and I'm trying to figure out whether it's a bet, or if he's gotten himself into some kind of woman trou-ble—a stage five clinger or something. Sage scans me through his signature droopy, ink blue eyes, and I swear my ovaries are singing a cappella at the sight of his jaw of steel. He should come with a book-long warning label. I'm half-tempted to Google a ques-tion about getting pregnant just by looking at him. Sage grabs the tip of my blanket, unplasters it from my body, and yanks me by the pajamas to straddle him. It happens so fast the oxygen leaves my lungs in a short *whoosh*. I'm panting now, on top of him, and his hands are on my ass, and I'm not stopping him. Why am I not stopping him? I know I should. He will break my heart and I'll have no one to blame but myself. I've seen it happen countless times be-fore. By the time we finished high school, eighty percent of the girls broke out in hives just from hearing his name.

"You'll still get free rent, but for as long as you're my fake girlfriend, I'll also pay the bills. You'll get free access to my truck—anytime you want. Last but not least: you'll get *me*. All of me. No other women. No distractions. No games. Just you and me, JoJo.

Because it's always been the two of us, and it's time we act this way, even if only for a little while."

He smells of wood and mint and a real Christmas tree. Like a sweet memory I want to cling onto. My limbs are lax and I know I'm making a huge mistake, but I'm done resisting. Believe me, I've tried. It brought me nowhere but to square one, salivating over my best friend.

I nod slowly. "Okay. What's the deadline?"

"End of May," he shoots, letting out a long sigh and placing his forehead to mine. It's intimate. So much more intimate than anything I'd ever done with the Brandons of the world, and I never stopped and debated whether I should date *them*. May is graduation month. Sage is offering me a free ride till the end of school. And let's not kid ourselves—I could use my waiting money for other things. Paying my student loan debt, getting a faster laptop. That kind of stuff.

We sit like this for a long minute before he cups my ass again and squeezes. It's so playful and friendly, I don't bark at him to stop.

"Welcome to couplehood, bae. We've got this."

Chapter
FOUR

Sage

"Hey, man, bad news."

For you, not for me, I'm tempted to add. Fucking fantastic news for me. I still can't believe she said yes. Then again, I'm not entirely sure she knew what this would entail. When I told JoJo I wanted to be her fake boyfriend, I meant it. We'll be doing things couples do. In bed, and the kitchen, and the bathroom, and even the fucking stairway, if we can't help ourselves.

"What's up?" Mark lifts his head, a towel wrapped around his waist. He slams his blue locker shut and uses a second towel to rub his black hair dry. Even though he's on my team, he's been riding the bench for the last year-and-a-half. I can't help but internally curse him. Who the hell does he think he is, checking out my JoJo? *Whoa.* My JoJo? She's not mine. Only that's not entirely true. She feels a lot like something no one else can ever have, so who the hell says she's not mine?

And if she isn't, I'm going to make her mine.

Because I'm done fucking around after what happened last month.

Done messing with a bunch of time-wasters while the Marks of the world are making moves on. My. Girl.

"So, Jolie and I are kind of together." I prop my shoulder against my own locker, looking down at him. God bless my late father. He gave me the height to tower over most motherfuckers who aren't signed with NBA teams.

Mark's eyes widen in disbelief before he schools his features and clears his throat like the good, rich boy that he is. "Oh, yeah?"

"Yep." I pop the P out with a grin.

"Let me get this straight. You slept with her this weekend, *after* I asked you for the one-hundredth time to sniff around for me?"

"Look," I say cuttingly, evading the question, "I've known this girl since we were ten." Since she promised me I'd always be a huge chunk of her world and I blossomed in her friendship, set roots in our companionship, and grew up to be someone strong. "This shit is not going away, so I suggest *you* move on."

"You're kind of a prick, you know that, Poirier?"

Oh, I know. Grew up with one. Became one. Vicious cycle, etc.

I clutch my navy football jersey and gasp loudly and comically, flattening my back against the row of lockers. "Now I'm butthurt. Which means that the only way I'll get over this is if you kiss my ass."

"Well," Mark says, his face red now, and I'm so going to find a way to kick him off of the team if he oversteps. I have that kind of power, and I'm not afraid to use it. "That's not going to happen."

"In that case, you better stay the fuck away from my girlfriend *and* me, yeah?"

He doesn't answer.

Just walks away.

I watch his back, and for the first time in my life, the taste of victory bursts on my tongue outside the football field. I savor it, my throat bobbing with a swallow. I know I was being an irrational prick to Mark. I know that. But I couldn't *stop* it.

This whole thing made me crazy, and as much as it put me low on the moral scale—because let's admit it, I had zero reason to feel bitter about any of this—my temper won. It won, and I lost.

I lost my cool.

I lost my patience.

Then I lost my control.

Where the fuck did all this come from?

What the hell is happening?

Jolie

What. The. Hell. Is. Happening?

I'm having the worst day of my *life*. It starts with Chelsea accidentally spilling her hot coffee on my white blouse—I don't have time to go back home and change between classes, so the stained shirt remains. It continues with my favorite professor gathering us in class and announcing her sudden departure due to a tragedy in the family, then sometime before noon, Mark Tensely, a guy I've been crushing on for six months now (silently, of course. I'm so shy I almost combusted when he came in the other day to return some of Sage's gear) came to ask Chelsea on a date, all while ignoring my existence.

By the time I get back home after a stop at the library, it's dark and Sage is waiting for me in the living room with two slices of pizza, a Caesar salad, and beers. I'm so relieved to see the food—and him—I nearly whimper at the beauty of having both of them.

This is what heaven looks like, right?

"Sit. I'll put some *X Factor* on." He pats the tangerine sofa he's slouched on. Clad only in gray running shorts, he is naked from the waist up, which is not surprising—Sage has a strict no-shirt policy around the house. I make my way over and plop down next to him with a sigh. He hits *Play* just as I take the first bite of my pizza.

"Nice blouse." His eyes are already dead on the screen.

"Thank…" I start, but then remember it has a coffee stain the size of Mississippi and frown. "I should probably take a shower and change before dinner." I've never felt too self-conscious in front of him before, but I do now.

"Bullshit. I'm your boyfriend. You don't have to doll-up for me. I like the real you. The girl who snores when she is tired and smells of garlic every Sunday after her grandmama's special casserole."

"You're my fake boyfriend," I correct, trying to set some boundaries.

"Irrelevant. Everything that came out of my mouth was real."

I roll my eyes and dig into my pizza and salad, internally admitting that my best friend will one day make a kick-ass real boyfriend, just probably not to me. Simon Cowell is slaying people in the auditions segment. Two girls cry and one guy threatens to sue him. Then the commercials come on and we both stretch out on the couch.

"Do your Simon Cowell impression for me." Sage elbows my ribs, winking at me playfully.

"Maybe later. I'm exhausted." I rub my eyes. Inhaling the pizza, salad, and beer like food is a foreign concept that's left me in a carbma (carb coma). Sage stares me down, his face intense yet unreadable.

"You know what'll happen if you refuse, right?"

I do. And I want it to happen. Shamefully, our tickle sessions are the most erotic thing in my life right now. I haven't had sex in months, and I swear there'd be cobwebs all over my vajayjay had I not purchased enough sex toys to open a store.

"I do not negotiate with terrorists," I say adamantly.

"So happy to hear, because I think I'm about done talking, anyway."

His eyes hone in on mine and his ripped body tenses before he pounces on me, tackling me to the carpeted floor. I fall with a bang, but his huge palm is covering the back of my head as it always does. He's on top of me. With me writhing beneath him. I'm pretending to fight him, throwing balled fists into his chest, waiting for the tickles to arrive, when…

"*Stop*," he breathes, and I notice that he is not moving. His pelvic bones are rubbing against mine, his erection is digging into my groin, and it is thick, and long, and tilted to the right. My mouth waters and my eyes gloss over. Jesus H, since when did my best friend become such a *man?*

"What?" I croak.

He leans forward, his mouth only inches from mine. His body heavy, his hard-on tantalizing, his scent breathtaking, he mouths into my lips, "Game change: if you want me to stop whatever it is I'm going to do as your fake boyfriend, say the name Simon Cowell."

I groan. He's giving me safe words now. I don't have to ink them onto my brain, because I know I'll never use them. His hips start to move, and he is sliding up and down, grinding himself against my needy pussy. I'm on fire, seeing stars, salivating at the intense friction. Every nerve in my body is buzzing with an impending orgasm, because it's been so long, *too* long, and I open my thighs for him, my denim digging into my clit and rubbing against it.

"Say Simon Cowell, or I'll continue." His voice is heavy and rough and raw. He is the kid I fell in love with at the age of ten, and the man I would give the world to at the age of twenty. I don't even care that he is probably using me. Using me as a fake girlfriend. Using me as a sexual outlet on this carpet.

I say nothing, because I'd die if he stops. Maybe not literally, but I'm pretty sure I'll be the proud owner of the very first case of female blue balls.

He increases his speed, dry-humping me, one forearm propped near my ear and his other hand sliding to my neck. I want him to kiss me. I don't want him to kiss me. I want us to break all the rules that helped us survive our turbulent childhood, that helped us defy *When Harry Met Sally*, that shows the world that men and women can't be friends. I want to obliterate our friendship on this carpet. I want to show him that my stupid, reckless, defiant heart only beats for him.

"Fuck, you're beautiful," he growls, squeezing my neck softly. His throbbing cock is pushing between my thighs, digging deeper into my slit, even through the denim, and I know it must be painful for him. He is half-penetrating me, and my eyes roll back despite my best intentions, the darkness behind them littered with stars and fireworks.

"Say it now, JoJo. Simon Cowell. Make me stop, or…" He leaves the sentence hanging in the air. *Or he'll take more.* But maybe I want more. He said this was going to feel real. Monogamous, even. And now that Mark Tensely is no longer an option (not that we were a thing, but he was a distraction from Sage), I might as well take him up on that offer.

If Sage thinks our friendship can survive it—or worse, that our friendship isn't worth keeping our hands to ourselves—who am I to disagree?

"Too scared to cross the line?" I hiss, my eyes widening at my own words. I've never taunted Sage about sex. About everything else? Sure. But not this. "I'm not sure what you're using me for, Sage, but if you're using me, I fully intend to use *you*."

The words barely leave my mouth before his mouth crashes down on mine, devouring me like a starved wolf. Like that boy who cried to the moon, and the moon finally answered back. It strikes me like lightning. Sage is *hungry*. And I'm his meal. His pouty lips drag against mine, seeking an opening. He captures my lower lip with his teeth and tug, tug, *tugs* until I have no choice but to part my lips and give him better access. His tongue is invading, ruling, and assaulting my own. It chases mine frantically, licks the walls of my mouth, moves across my teeth, memorizing every single spot in my mouth. My eyes roll in pleasure when he takes my tongue between his lips and sucks on it hard, shoving his hand into my jeans. I'm not sure at what point he pulled down my zipper, but now he is rubbing my swollen, sensitive clit through my panties while he's devouring my mouth, our tongues dancing seductively with one another. My whole body shakes uncontrollably.

"Please. Oh my God. Sage."

It's too much. The unexpected, sudden gratification. Don't get me wrong—I make it a point to get myself off three times a week to keep myself sane, but I can't remember the last time my body danced on its own accord with passion and delirious need. It occurs to me that I'm about to come before he's even pulled off his running shorts, so I try to make him slow down by saying our very ridiculous safe word.

"Simo…"

His lips leave mine and he covers my mouth with his palm to keep me silent while he rises to his knees, pulling his shorts down with his free hand.

He shakes his head on a smirk. "If you want me to stop, just say no, JoJo. But from this point forward, you're not screaming anyone's name but mine. Do you want me to stop?" He takes his hand away and I grab him by the wrist and graze his knuckle with my teeth before slipping the tip of his finger between my lips and giving it a little suck.

Hell no, I don't want him to stop.

His thick cock springs out of his shorts, and he presses the long, hot, velvety shaft against my bare stomach. My blouse rode up sometime during this spontaneous make-out session, and now Sage is tugging it further up to accommodate his cock, resting it on the little pink bow at the center of my bra, before reaching under me to snatch my bra, tearing it apart.

"Gonna tit-fuck you now. Been wanting to do

that since your thirteenth birthday. Remember the day? Checkered baby blue dress, ham on rye in the meadow, showing me the first sign of tits..." He drags his tongue across my chin, closing in on my mouth with a sloppy kiss. A kiss with too much tongue. Too much saliva. Too much *everything*, yet not enough of him. My response is squeezing my breasts together around his thick cock. The pad of his thumb is rubbing my clit again, and my quivering thighs begin to jerk uncontrollably. He pinches my clit. I moan so loudly my ears ring. *Pinch, pinch, pinch*. After a dozen small pinches, I feel a tug on the invisible string of pleasure that connects us. I explode when he finally pinches harder, sending me over the edge. I writhe under my best friend, shouting his name with the kind of wild abandon I hadn't felt since the day I ran toward him in the pouring hot rain.

I barely have time to come down from my orgasm before he starts fucking my tits, the tip of his cock poking my chin every time he grinds himself on my torso. He scoots up, sitting on my stomach with his knees on either side of me. His muscular thighs harden, holding most of his weight as he goes at it like a professional porn star.

"Look at me," he growls like a wounded animal, his tone far from its usual playfulness. I raise my head. My hazels meet his blues. He smirks the most patronizing, jerk-fueled smile I've ever seen, cupping my cheeks with one hand.

"I want to come in your mouth."

I nod silently. I've never given anyone oral sex. Not that I have anything against it, but I guess I never felt super comfortable enough with any of my past boyfriends. But Sage is not just a guy I went on a few dates with. He is the boy who kicked other boys' asses when they disrespected me at school—despite my telling him that I could take care of myself—and tried (and failed) to bake me shortbread cookies every Christmas because he knew they were my favorite.

He is good enough to never mention it if I suck (not literally), and man enough to never say a word about it to anyone we know.

"Oh, fuck, so close. Jolie, my beautiful, gorgeous Jolie…"

He scoots up, slides his cock from between my tits, and shoves it into my mouth, cupping my head from behind and making me deep throat him. And I do. I fight my gag reflex and wrap my lips around his cock as he pumps the base, warm, thick liquid sliding down my throat in spurts. My hands are on his rear, and I'm squeezing hard, as if I'm the one who is milking him, and it feels dirty and wrong and so magnificently right.

When he collapses next to me, his salty taste on

my lips and tongue, I close my eyes and breathe, trying to rearrange the jumbled mess that is my mind. My bra is torn, my pussy throbs and burns from the friction of the denim and the pinching, and I feel like a train wreck with smeared lipstick.

A big paw reaches across my stomach, rolls me over to my side, and embraces me into a hug. Sage kisses my temple—like a loving friend, not like a quick lay—and whispers something I cannot decipher.

"What did you say?" I murmur, allowing my head to rest on his iron pecs.

He doesn't answer, and I don't probe, falling asleep in the arms of the boy I pieced back together myself with a hug.

Sage

The next day, I tackle Mark to the ground in practice. My official reason? He's a fucker. My *real* reason? Jolie is standing across the football field with Chelsea and a few of her other girlfriends, hugging her MacBook to her chest and laughing at something one of them said. That, in itself is not a problem. But the fact that Mark just ogled her for two straight minutes? Totally is.

"What part of 'she's mine' did you not get?" I snarl in his face, nailing him to the ground. Well, this escalated quickly. Can't help it, though. The more I think about how much of a dickbag this dude is for even suggesting he'd date my best friend, the more I want to punch him into unconsciousness. Luckily, Jolie and I have this kind of relationship where we don't even have to fully explain ourselves to each other and she'd agreed to "date" me.

Just like I'd agreed to take care of her friend's pet ferret for a month junior year because her grandmama was allergic and she couldn't do it herself. We're there for each other in big ways and little ones. Always.

"I'm not looking at Jolie, dickwad! I'm looking at Chelsea. I asked her out yesterday." Mark pushes me off of him, and I roll on the hot, damp grass, laughing to the bright blue sky. It unburdens me from weight I didn't know I had on my heart. Ever since I graduated from high school, I've always had it easy—easy with girls, easy with grades, and easy with football. The rest I didn't really care about, frankly. And maybe that's why I've never had something I was in danger of losing. I do now, and hell if it's not a bitch to keep it from slipping between my fingers.

"Chelsea, huh? You move fast," I note, standing to my feet and wobbling between Michael and Elliott, who are stretching on the ground.

"Said the guy who dicked the girl I wanted to date just so I couldn't have her." Mark picks his gear up from the grass and stomps toward the dressing room behind me. He catches up to me, and I rein in the urge to steal a glance at my fake girlfriend, who really doesn't feel that fake at all.

"Don't talk about her like that." I scowl.

"Why? You talk about girls like that all the time." He laughs.

Because she's not a fucking girl; she's my best friend, I'm tempted to yell, but I'm not five, nor a pussy, so I bite my lip and change the subject.

"You inviting Chelsea to that charity thing in New York?" I jerk my chin in the girls' direction. One of my sponsors is flying me out with a plus one. I can't wait to see Jolie in a red dress—that's the dress code for the female attendees—and seeing everyone's faces when this Southern belle is on my arm alone could make me shoot my load all over my tux.

"Why? Are you asking Jolie?"

"Of course, I fucking am. She's my girl. So?" I don't know why I'm pushing this. Maybe because I really want to hear that he's over JoJo.

"Fuck knows, man. We haven't even gone on one date. What's it to you?" He frowns and stops by our blue lockers. I shrug. I know that Mark and Jolie don't speak to each other. I'd just like to keep it that way for the remainder of our last year of college. If she finds out I cockblocked her out of this potential relationship, she is going to jerk me off with a Brillo pad.

"Just curious."

"Hey, man, don't take this the wrong way, but it looks like something's eating you," Mark says carefully, peeling his shirt off and throwing it on a bench behind us. "Is everything okay?"

Everything is not okay. I made a horrible mistake with a girl, and even though it made me realize that there's another girl I deeply want and love, I hurt someone. A lot. But I just smile. "Couldn't be more perfect."

"Good." He strokes his chin. "Good."

I take my clothes off and step into the shower, letting the scorching hot water punish me for what I did.

I'll fix it all.

Fix it all with Jolie.

Jolie

The day drags.

By the time I stumble through my front door, it's already ten at night.

Between my shift at the Happy Bunny—a diner off of Bordeaux Street—and a library session with Chelsea and Penny, I'm thoroughly spent. Too exhausted to even grab myself a bite. The minute I get into the apartment, I head straight to the shower, scrub off the day's dirt, slip into my pajamas (conveniently located on a hanger in the bathroom right next to my towel to avoid any more embarrassing hallway encounters with Sage) and slide under my blanket without even turning on the lamp next to my bed. I scoot to the edge of my bed and close my eyes.

Mmm, this is nice.

So relaxing.

I can just drift and clear my mind and not think about...

Okay, something is poking my ass.

Correction: an erection is poking my ass.

Double correction: a *bare* erection is. Poking. My. Ass. *Mothertrucker!*

"Sage!" I jolt, partly pissed, but—let's admit it—mostly turned on. It's like Sage has the manual to my body and knows how to work it better than I do. Which is weird. We still haven't spoken about the sudden escalation in our relationship, but since it's already happened—what's crossing another line, right?

"Shhh, baby girl." His strong, warm palm slides down to cup my ass. "Let Daddy take care of you."

"Call yourself my daddy one more time and I'm fishing your eyeballs out with a spoon."

"Fuck, my girl has some pent-up aggression in her. So glad I'm here to loosen..." He glides the sleeve of my pajama dress across my shoulder and kisses it. "Her." He lets the gown slip over my head and down my body, leaving me completely naked, save for my cotton panties. "Up." His hand slinks between my thighs, cups my pussy, and squeezes. *Hard.*

"No need, as I'm perfectly loose," I murmur, teasing him. He slides my panties down and I wiggle my ass into his erection so that his cock is halfway between my ass cheeks, putting pressure on my tight hole. He could dream. But then again, that's exactly what I want him to do. Crave me like a fantasy.

"Nah, you're not loose. Tight as your sweet little cunt, more like." His tongue skates down my spine, leaving shivers in its wake. He is moving south. Who gave him permission to move south? This is like *Game of Thrones*. Wars should be fought to win the south. You can't just knock on the door and expect me to open it up.

Wait, you totally can if you look like Sage Poirier.

"Too tired for sex, Mr. Fake Boyfriend. I'm not in the mood to move," I protest one last time, just to tell myself that I've tried if things go wrong. Just to show myself that I really did try, I flip the lamp on for emphasis, like I'm going to be reading, or watching TV, or not thinking about having sex with my best friend (lie).

"That's okay. I skipped my carbs today, Miss *Real*

41

Girlfriend. I think I'll just feast on you."

Real girlfriend? Don't dwell on it. He'd say anything to get into your panties right now.

"I think my juices are more, like, protein," I blab. I should probably shut up.

"No such thing as too much protein in an athlete's diet. Better go down there. Maybe even come back for a second serving later tonight." He cups my face with one hand and twists my head around so he can kiss me. Our tongues find each other and do a happy dance together. My nipples tighten and pucker from the heat between my legs and the chilly breeze of the room and he twists one of them between his fingers. Then he lets go and slides under my blanket, where I can't see him.

Sage throws my legs open and settles between them. He doesn't say anything at first, and my self-consciousness kicks in. I know my pussy is perfectly normal. Waxed—every part tucked in like a virgin rose right before blooming—smooth to a fault and bubblegum pink. Everything is where it should be. So why is he not saying anything? Maybe he is suffocating under the blanket. I should check how he is doing. This is one obituary I wouldn't want to make.

'Died between my legs from lack of oxygen on the same day I had a tuna melt for lunch...'

Oh, God. I forgot about the tuna melt.

"Sage?" I murmur, scooting upward. He pins me down by my hipbones in one, swift movement, throwing my legs even wider.

"Shut up," he says from under the blanket, this mammoth of a man shifting beneath the soft fabric. "JoJo? I think we need to break up our fake relationship."

My eyes flare and my cheeks flush red. "Why?"

"Because I just fell in love. I'm talking love at first sight. Your pussy is just so darn pretty, I wanna marry it. Can I marry your pussy? The rest of your body can stay single, I swear."

I laugh and playfully swat what I'm guessing is his head—or his shoulder, both are super hard and round.

"If you love her so much, you should give her some TLC. Show her how you really feel," I encourage, biting my lower lip on a smile.

"Can I kiss her? Or does she not kiss on a first date?"

"She definitely does. She's a little hussy."

I feel his tongue flattening against the base of my pussy, right next to my crack, and tremble at the sudden wet and warm sensation.

"Call her a hussy one more time, and I'm kicking you out of this ménage."

"You can't do that. I'm attached to her." This is getting ridiculous. But also so much fun. Sage uses

43

his fingers to open me wide and plunges his tongue into me, penetrating me with his tongue all the way in, and I moan loudly and clutch his head under the blanket. "Oh, my God!"

"Fuck, she's an even better kisser than you," Sage says. I swat his head lightly again as he starts working me relentlessly under the cover. Thrusting his tongue into me, in and out, all while using his thumb to rub my clit in delicious circles that make me want to shed happy tears.

"Yes, that's it. Oh, Sage. Oh, Sage. Oh…"

I'm getting close, and he knows it, because he pins my thighs to the bed, not letting me deny him access to my most sensitive part. Since his hands are now busy, he uses the tip of his straight nose to rub my clit in circles as he continues to fuck me with his tongue.

"Take back what you said." His voice is dark and serious, so far away from the best friend I know and love. And yet, this voice is no longer strange to me. This is how my lover sounds. The man I want to sleep with, and do very unfriendly, yet nice things to.

"A…about what?" I stutter on my own carnal desire.

"About your pussy being a hussy. She's not a fucking hussy. She opens up and sings, but just for me. She's a slut, but just for me. She's a fucking horny maniac—for. No. One. But. Me. Yeah?"

Jesus H, his dirty talk game is strong. I nod to myself, swallowing, feeling the hot wave of a climax washing over me, starting from the crown of my head and moving down like a wave to the rest of my body. I'm quivering, shaking like a leaf.

After I come, he glides up in one smooth movement, reappearing from under the blanket. His face is flushed pink, and his lips are glistening with my arousal. Aaaand…he looks like that boy I fell in love with again. So vulnerable and broken and unbelievably youthful. It messes with my head, and I wonder if he feels the same. Like he is treading on a tightrope between familiarity and grown-up games.

"Tell me she is mine," he whispers. I blink. It takes me a second to realize that he is talking about my pussy. *Again.* I grin.

"Is Sage Junior mine?" I reach beneath us to cup his hard-on. He is butt naked under the covers, and I want to see and taste everything.

"He is yours. I am yours. We're both yours. If…" Pause. Beat of silence. Visible swallow. "If you'll have us."

He sounds serious. So, so serious. But I know him well enough to recognize that Sage is a total people-pleaser and cocky to a fault. I have to remind myself that he'll say whatever it is I want to hear and breeze through it without thinking about the consequences to get what he wants. Truth be told, he's never had a serious girlfriend and never brought the same girl to our apartment twice. I remind myself, therefore, that this is a game. A game that will end come May, and with it, our whole relationship will never be the same again. Sage will get drafted somewhere cool and exotic and will become filthy rich, and I'll continue my small-town life here in Louisiana. The probability of it all slams into my chest all at once, like a cold bucket of ice.

This is all temporary.

The reality is, he wants a fake girlfriend until May, because after May, he'll be gone to Boston or California, making a career. He just wants some kind of girlfriend experience before he goes so he doesn't feel like he's missing out.

He will use me.

And will *dump* me.

He. Will. Forget. About. Me.

And every time I witness him visiting his mama across the road, on Christmas or Thanksgiving, I'll remember being a notch on his miles-long belt.

I swallow, the back of my eyeballs stinging with unshed tears.

"Simon Cowell," I croak, my voice barely audible. His eyebrows drop into a shocked frown, his lips parting in disbelief.

"JoJo?"

"*Simon Cowell,*" I repeat, raising my shaky voice. "Please," I add.

He rolls off of me, propping his head on his forearm and watching me. My heart stutters as I scurry to the edge of the bed, throw my nightgown on, suddenly forgetting about being tired and hungry and *happy*, and pad my way to the kitchen.

Don't look back, don't look back, don't look back.

In the kitchen, I open the freezer and take out the Cherry Garcia Ben and Jerry's. This is Sage we're talking about, not Brandon. He is totally worth the calories. I prop my lower body against the counter, shoving spoonfuls of ice cream down my throat, not even bothering to taste it. My back is to the hallway so I don't see him. But I *feel* him. His big steps. His commanding body. The heat rolling off his muscular frame.

"What the fuck was that all about, JoJo?" he asks behind me. He doesn't sound pissed off at all. Just sad and…disappointed. God, the idea of disappointing him after everything we've been through is nothing short of agonizing. We promised each other so much, and kept good on those promises. I don't want this to change. I don't want *us* to change.

"I can't be your fake girlfriend anymore."

"But…"

I turn around and meet his gaze, my vision slicing right through all the pain that's swimming in his blues. I don't want to see it. Facing it will undo every logical decision I need to make right now. He is wearing a tight pair of black boxers, an Adonis with a sculpted face, asking for his mortal friend to play a game only the gods can win.

"Simon Cowell," I say one last time. "Please let go."

He shakes his head, turns around, and walks away, doing exactly as I tell him to.

Chapter
SIX

Sage

The next day, I do the unthinkable—the un-fucking-doable, and push a teammate to the ground because he stretched too close to me. Yep, I shit you not. Quarterbacks usually try to protect their hands and arms, not shove them into other footballers' personal space to start a fight.

"What the fuck is your problem?!" Michael asks, throwing his helmet to the grass and shoving my chest. I'm just looking for an excuse to rearrange some random dipshit's face, so this is all the invitation I need to get in his personal space and growl, "You've been asking for this, motherfucker!"

I'm about to throw a punch—knowing that it's going to put me in a very bad spot, knowing that scouters are roaming the training area, knowing that I could be flushing my whole future down the toilet—when I feel a big hand yanking me away from Michael. Tom and Dre are pushing Michael in the other direction while Mark is hugging my midsection and dragging me to the other end of the field. Lines of mud are forming beneath my feet. I've always been an aggressive player. Comes with the territory of being a huge-ass kid with a shit ton of issues. I was actually supposed to be an O-Liner. But it so happened that my first coach said I was too intelligent not to be a quarterback and forced me into the position. Today, I'm feeling especially confrontational. The kind of asshole that needs to be thrown inside the octagon or ring with Conor McGregor and Floyd Mayweather and can still come out of there unscathed.

"Are you trying to shit all over your future?" Mark bares his teeth, slamming me against the wall of the sports auditorium. I shrug, taking off my helmet and running my paw through my now long-ish hair. I normally ask Jolie to cut it for me, but I've been too busy trying to get in her pants lately to ask her to take care of that shit.

"It's fine. He won't say a word to Coach Drescher." I wave Mark off. He puts his hands on his waist and paces in front of me like an exasperated parent. Behind him, my teammates are arguing and yelling and *I did this shit*. The realization leaves a bitter taste in my mouth.

"Doesn't matter, bro. You're still acting like King Douche of Cuntland, and you need to cut that shit before you get blacklisted. You can't afford to do that. Not when you're so close to getting drafted."

I know he's right. I also know that I've been acting like a dick all day, and that's unlike me. I need to get my head back in the game, but it's hard when I know that JoJo's a few feet away, going about her day after smashing my fucking heart yesterday on the kitchen floor.

"So, I shouldn't be a massive dick to everyone even though I have a massive dick. Gotcha." I nod, trying to lighten up the mood. Mark lifts his head and pins me with a serious look.

"What's gotten into you? Something's wrong?"

Like I'd ever tell him.

"Nothing's wrong. Everything's so dandy and fucking right I want to break into a dance." The sarcasm drips from my mouth like drool.

"Yeah? So this has nothing to do with you and Jolie?" He lifts one lonely brow.

Her mere name on his lips makes me want to punch the wall behind me, then run a fucking marathon to spend all the pent-up aggression coursing through my body.

"Everything's great between JoJo and me. Don't say her name again, please."

Mark stares at me, dumbfounded. A smile spreads across his lips. We're not super tight, Mark and I, but I know that he is good people. I also know that he was born and raised in a nice Southern family where people hug a lot and talk about feelings and shit. That makes me uncomfortable around him sometimes. Like he can see through me. See the parts I'm only really comfortable sharing with JoJo.

"You're in love with her," he says, chuckling. "Holy shit, man. You are in love with your roommate. That's hilarious. Does she know?"

Does JoJo know? Maybe the better question is—do *I* know? Sure, yeah, I like her, but what, exactly, does it mean? Fuck, I can't even seem to read myself anymore. Why else would I act the way I do? Like the Duke of Dickwads. But admitting to myself that I'm in love—*not just love, but in love*—with my best friend is somehow like admitting defeat. Because other than a couple times recently, JoJo has never flirted with me in her entire life, and I'm pretty sure if I ever told her how I feel, she'd laugh in my face and tell me it's a phase.

It's not a phase.

It's here to stay.

I'm in love with my best friend.

With the girl who ran in the rain for me.

With the girl who did my homework all the way through elementary and high school so I could concentrate on my football, and gave me pointers and summaries when we walked to school together every day.

With the girl who believed in me before even *I* believed in myself.

And showed up at my games every weekend, her textbooks on her lap, doing homework in-between cheering for me.

I'm in love with my roommate.

With the girl who cuts my hair and knows my favorite color is black and my favorite food is Cajun fried catfish.

With the proud owner of the sweetest pussy in Louisiana.

I'm in love with Jolie Louis.

And I'm going to conquer her. Consequences be damned.

Jolie

"I just had the best date of *life* yesterday. Not an exaggeration. A fact," Chelsea swoons, throwing her arms across the library desk and burying her head between them. She blows a lock of raven hair from her face. Her cheeks are pink, her eyes are bloodshot, and her huge smile is telling me that she is crushing hard, all while riding the mother of all natural highs. I sit across from her, smiling as I rearrange my sensible blouse. I've always pegged myself as a maternal chick. It's not the most feminist thing in the world to admit, but I already know my most rewarding role in life will be being a mom. But Chelsea? She's something else. She aspires to become a nanny after we graduate. Save up for a few years before becoming a mother herself. She's got a wedding and (at least) four kids on her (utterly crazy) brain twenty-four-freaking-seven.

"Where did Mark take you?" I probe, pretending to be typing on my MacBook. Really, I'm just stalling and trying to look like everything is okay. Like I'm not a mess of epic proportions. Sage and I haven't spoken a word to each other today. No texting. No stumbling together, laughing in the hallway. Even the drive to campus was silent. He tapped the wheel, I texted my mama, and liked every single thing my friends posted on Facebook. It was awkward to say the least.

"We had a picnic under the stars. Then we went to my place. Nikki is gone for the week, so we had the place to ourselves. We watched *Suicide Squad*. Then we…" She blushes, looking away. "Then we did other stuff. And, so, yeah, he's a great guy."

"I'm so happy for you." And I am. A friendship ain't worth the time you spend together unless you can wholeheartedly feel the joy and love your peer experiences when something amazing happens to them.

"Thank you, sweets. So, what about you? Still mad about that jackass, Brandon? You should really put yourself out there more, lady. Guys will be lining up as soon as you give them the signal you're interested." She wiggles her brows and closes her thick textbook. I offer her a weak smile, looking around us to make sure the library is deserted. It is. I haven't told her about the whole fake relationship with Sage yet. I kind of figured it would run its course before we even had the chance to explore it, as with many of Sage's crazy ideas. I was even partly right. True, I did most of the ruining of said fake relationship, but it doesn't matter. Not really. I don't, however, want to keep anything from Chelsea.

"I kind of hooked up with Sage this past week. Nothing too serious. We just messed around." I drum my collarbone with my fingers.

"I know," she says, straight-faced. I raise an eyebrow.

"What?"

"Dude, I know, Penny knows, every single person on campus knows," she reports nonchalantly, downing the rest of her latte and throwing the cup into the trash at the side of our desk, shrugging. "Mark and I talked about it. Sage told him. Apparently, he told the whole football team that if they as much as breathe in your direction, he'd cut their noses off. Kind of possessive, if you ask me. Never thought he was the caveman type."

I'm staring at Chelsea with my mouth agape, realizing that it's not a good look, and yet too shocked to respond coherently.

I look around me. There is only one more desk occupied in the whole library other than Chelsea's and mine. It's a bunch of sorority girls sitting across the room with their feathery pink pens and white, lush cardigans and blonde, high ponytails. They're staring at me, and I know why. If eyes could stab, I'd be bleeding to death on the floor. To them, Sage is not a real person, with a story, a personal tragedy, and complex personality traits. He's a legend. A status symbol. Like a Ferrari or a Versace item. Fierce protectiveness grips my throat. I don't know how I'd be able to live if I ever found out that he got married to this type of girl. The ones who see him for so much less than who he is.

"Earth to Jolie." Chelsea waves her little hands in front of me, smiling. I snap out of my stupor, shaking my head lightly.

"Sorry, you were saying?" I close my MacBook and grab my shoulder bag from under my chair. I admit defeat. There's just no way I'll be able to concentrate on anything other than him today.

"So things must be serious between you and Sage, if he is claiming you as his in front of the entire world." We both stand up, gather our belongings, and make our way to the door. I'm about to answer Chelsea, when…

"Slut," one of the sorority girls coughs into her curled fist, just as I pass her by.

"Social climber," the other one breathes viciously. I keep walking, ignoring them, but just as I'm about to round the corner into the hallway, I notice that Chelsea is no longer by my side. I turn my head around and see her standing in front of their desk. My eyes nearly bug out of their sockets, cartoon-style. *Oh, no.* Chelsea has some serious mama-bear-on-steroids-when-aunt-flow-is-in-town bones in her. She takes care of her own and never passes down a chance to stand up for a friend. But this bitch doesn't deserve her attention. Not one bit.

"Hey, girls." Chelsea juts one hip out, her hand on her hip and her smile Type 2 diabetes sweet as she snaps a picture of them with her phone. "Just wanted to stop by and let you know that by talking shit about the captain of the football team's girlfriend, you pretty much killed every opportunity you've ever had to date a jock in this place. Just putting it out there. So, good luck and so forth." My friend shrugs, strutting her way back to me.

"You didn't have to do that," I blurt, but still squeeze her into an embrace, my arm wrapped around her shoulder. We walk out to the orange and pink fall, toward the students' parking lot.

"I know I didn't, but I wanted to. So, are you and Sage a thing, or what?" She stops by her sensible blue Buick and fishes out the keys from her back pocket.

"Um, no. I kind of got freaked out yesterday at the possibility of him leaving the state in May and basically told him I'm calling things off. It all started with him telling me that he wanted me to be his fake girlfriend until graduation. Something about a Christmas event in New York, or something, so I think his telling people that we're an item is more because of his mysterious plan and less about a love declaration," I sullenly admit. Chelsea whips her head and gives me her best are-you-a-complete-idiot expression. It's a cross between puzzled and annoyed.

"You seriously think he's playing a game? You don't know that he likes you?"

I shake my head. I mean, I do. I know Sage likes me a lot as a friend. It's hard not to see it. We do so much for each other. But more than that? Romantically other than a lay? Nah. He had countless chances to ask me out, to blur the lines, to take a chance. Literally, a decade of opportunities ticked by. He saw me with boyfriends. On dates. At prom with Clay Jacobs. He never gave me any indication that he was even remotely jealous. No reason he caught a bad case of the feels all of a sudden.

"Jolie, he is crazy about you."

"I don't see it."

"Well, you should, because everyone else does."

I bite my lower lip and ponder. Maybe it's true. Maybe I'm just being a bit of a bitch. I mean, what exactly am I expecting from him right now? A declaration that he'll always be mine? A goddamn ring? Who knows what's going to happen in May? All we have is today, and today matters.

"Okay, I'll talk to him," I say. Chelsea nods.

"I'll give you a ride to work." She winks.

"You're the best." And for the millionth time since I met her here a couple of years ago, I thank the Lord that He gave me one best friend that I love like a drug, and another who takes care of me like a fairy.

Chapter
SEVEN

Jolie

I tie my yellow apron around my waist in the employees' room of the Happy Bunny. Trisha, my fifty-something-year-old colleague, coughs in my face, cigarette smoke drifting from her breath.

"All I'm sayin' is, don't let a man fool ya. They're all the same, hotcakes. They will use you and leave you if you let them. Why buy the cow if you can get the milk for free? See what I mean?" She gathers phlegm and spits it into a trash can, her fire engine red curly hair littered with white cigarette ash. I pretend to fluff her mane when really, I'm just making sure she doesn't lose all her tips *and* her job by sprinkling ash into people's food like a Tinkerbell from hell.

"Yep." I smile at her, not entirely sure why we're

talking about this. I haven't told her a word about Sage. I was actually trying to strike up a conversation about the weather. Trish leaves the darkened room to yell at our manager-slash-diner-owner, Travis, and I immediately fish out my phone, texting my best friend. The one I left hanging.

Me: Let's talk tonight?

He answers after less than five seconds.

Sage: Sure. Pick you up from work at eleven?

Me: Trish is giving me a ride back. She wants to talk about colleges bc her son is applying. I'll see you at home?

Sage: K. Chilling at Barnie's with the guys, but I'll be there on time. Everything good?

Me: Yeah. I just think I owe you an apology for freaking out on you yesterday like that.

Sage: Honestly, the only thing I'm worried about is how it's going to affect my relationship with your pussy, AKA my fiancée.

Me: So funny.

Sage: Also: so true.

Sage: But seriously, I don't know what happened yesterday. Whatever it was, I want to get it fixed. You're a part of my blood. I can't change my DNA, but I sure as hell can change everything else to keep you close. Yeah?

This man. *This. Man.* Maybe Chelsea is right. Maybe I'm not seeing what's so obviously clear to everyone else. Maybe Sage does like me in the same way that I like him.

Me: I hope you mean it.

Sage: I hope you know it. Speak soon x

The shift passes by in a blur. I don't think I've ever made such great tips, even though I pretty much work on autopilot. I don't feel tired or stressed or anxious. I'm just excited to see Sage at the end of my shift. Or maybe things go smoothly because business is so slow. Five hours into my shift, Travis saunters across the checkered black and white linoleum floors, braces one forearm over a red-hot booth, and slaps Trish's ass with a loud smack. "Trish, Jol, take the rest of the night off. Split the tips in the jar. This place is deader than my old man.

And he's dead, all right. Has been dead for twenty years now."

Insert: awkward giggle.

We nearly jump up and down with excitement and jog our way to Trish's piece-of-trash car (her words, not mine). She calls her old puke-green Ford Aerostar Bob after the asshole who ran away from her when she was eight months pregnant with his kid. Luckily, Bob's son is now seventeen and applying to colleges. A very different guy from his deadbeat dad.

"Where to?" Trish asks me when she gets behind the wheel, immediately lighting up a cigarette. She fluffs her hair, staring at the rearview mirror, and between us is an ashtray with enough cigarette butts to fill a bucket. I start giving her my address before realizing that Sage is not going to be there yet. So I give her the address for Barnie's, a converted barn turned into a sleazy bar all the jocks frequently hang out in.

"Aw, Barnie's. I have so many memories from that place. Most of them consisting of broken condoms, but still." Trish sighs, starts her car, and we're on a roll.

All the way to Barnie's, I'm answering questions about college when really, I'm an emotional, anxious mess. The idea that I might've pushed the one guy I wanted more than life itself away sits heavy in the back of my head and slowly opens a well of dark thoughts. Then I remember how sweet he was when we texted and take a deep breath.

By the time Trish's car comes to a stop in front of the old red barn with the Arctic Monkey's "I Bet You Look Good on the Dancefloor" leaking from between the door and windows, I'm a sweaty mess.

"Go ahead. I have a phone call to make. I'll wait for you in case he's already left." She cranes her neck, as if she's trying to see Sage through the windows. Okay, weird, but also totally appreciated. I haven't even mentioned I was meeting a guy here, though Trish is that kind of woman. One who can smell men from miles away.

"Thanks, Trish. You're the best." I squeeze her into a hug and hop out of the car. My knees are shaking as I make my way to the door. No one gets carded at Barnie's, because the place is in the middle of nowhere. It's almost underground. I could walk in there with a newborn and no one would bat an eye. No one would also try to rub themselves all over me, so maybe I *should* consider walking in with a baby if I ever feel like a drink but not like swatting off horny college boys.

"Jolie!" I spot Sage's teammates in the corner of the bar. Michael is the one who perks up the most, removing his arms from the counter he was plastered over and waves for me to come close. "Over here, pretty lady."

I also spot Tom, Mark, and Dre all sitting beside him, so I'm guessing the party is very much still alive and Sage should be nearby. I walk over to them, the smile on my face at odds with how I feel about wearing my orange and yellow Happy Bunny uniform of buttoned-down mini-dress and black stockings. Tom whistles as I go, and Mark smacks the back of his neck. My smile fades as I realize Sage is nowhere to be seen. I stop by the bar, my shoulder almost brushing Mark's, and he takes two large steps back and frowns. *Weirdo*. I know he's with Chelsea. Does he really think I'm going to hit on him?

"Where's Sage?" I ask in everyone's general direction, parking my forearms on the counter. Michael raises his eyebrows silently, his lips pursed. Tom looks the other way, Dre actually whistles as he pretends to text, and Mark is the only person who clears his throat and has the decency to make eye contact with me.

"Did he know you were coming?"

"No, why would he…" I begin to ask, when a high-pitched voice pierces through the air, that's heavy with warm, stinky alcohol and men's aftershave. *A girly* voice. I swivel my head on an instinct and watch Sage standing in front of one of the sorority girls Chelsea approached earlier this afternoon at the library.

The blondest one.

The prettiest one.

The one with the whitest, silkiest cardigan.

The one who called me a slut.

I want to see him tell her that this can't happen. That it will never happen. I want him to turn his back to her and walk over to me, like in the movies. I want her to chase him, and I want him to block her. These thoughts are not kind or noble, but they're coming from my deepest, most intimate part. The part who's seen him playing around with so many girls from the sidelines, wishing he'd just give me a chance. But, to my horror, he doesn't do any of those things. *She's* the one running away toward the door, and *he's* the one chasing after her.

"Amber, no, please!" he calls.

Amber.

No.

Please.

Sage never begs. Sage never pleads. Not to me and not to anyone.

He chases after her. I stay rooted to the floor. I watch the door swinging back and forth with the force of Amber's push. He's trailing behind.

He catches her.

He's holding her.

He's *hugging* her.

Their images are blurry through the dirty,

cloudy windows. I see their shapes dancing together through the dull glass and the mist of tears on my eyeballs. The way Amber pushes him away. The way he keeps on moving toward her. The sheer desperation in his body language. And that's when I feel Mark's hand on my shoulder.

"I don't know what it's about," he says, his voice quivering slightly, "but give him the benefit of the doubt."

A lonely tear escapes my right eye and runs down my cheek, free-falling into its end and splashing on the tip of my Chucks. I hear the guys shuffling and talking behind me, but can't distinguish what they're saying. My legs carry me to Amber and Sage. To the girl who called me a slut and to the guy who said I was in his blood but ran after someone else.

They're standing outside the barn. She's yelling at him. He looks miserable. The only good thing about this shitshow of a situation? Trish's car is still parked at the non-existent curb near the hay, the engine purring, as she talks on the phone, smoking a cigarette and staring at herself through the rearview mirror.

"Oh, great. Now your new girlfriend is here!" Amber shrieks, throwing her arms in the air on an eye roll. Then she huffs. I think I made my opinion about huffing clear. I narrow my eyes at the not-so-happy couple. Sage turns around instantly, his eyes growing wide.

"What are you doing here, JoJo?" The words struggle out of his mouth.

"Standing in your way, obviously. Don't worry, Sage. I'll make myself scarce so you can go back to your…" I frown at both of them, standing so close to each other, "business."

"No, wait. There's no business with Amber. No business at all. You don't understand…" He charges after me, but I take hurried steps toward Trish's car, swing the passenger door open, slide in, and nudge her to start driving. She does. She throws the lit cigarette out the window and pushes the gas pedal like we're on a police chase. I'm not sure I want to know how she mastered these escaping skills.

"Trouble with the boy?" Her voice is exceptionally cheerful, like she just proved a point. I shake my head, crossing my arms over my chest. I want to move out. I *need* to move out. I hate him. I want to kill him. I want to kiss him. I love him. I don't know what I'm feeling. Everything is wrong and twisted and final. Or maybe nothing happened at all and this has a very simple, logical explanation. I'm confused. I need to drink. I have to think about this sober.

Goddammit.

My phone starts pinging with messages as I see

Sage's burgundy truck careening after us. Well, that's just dandy.

Sage: Where are you going? Who is in the car with you?

Sage: You can't just leave. I didn't know you were coming. I can explain.

Sage: I know it looks bad.

Sage: You need to answer me, JoJo.

Sage: FUCK JOJO FUCK.

"Where to?" Trish asks, lighting her four-hundredth cigarette for the day as we speed toward an intersection. She nonchalantly passes a stop sign and I'm about to pee my pants—yeah, despite all the Pilates.

"Slow down, Trish."

"Did he cheat?" She ignores me, getting all worked up. "It looks like he's been cheatin' on ya. This kinda thing doesn't fly with me. Bob cheated."

"It's complicated, but…" *I don't want to die. Not even over Sage.*

"Bastard!" She hits the accelerator so hard my

head swings back. Meanwhile, the texts flow like cheap alcohol at a frat party.

Sage: Tell her to stop the goddamn vehicle or I swear I'll slam into you from the side to pull you over.

Sage: Bitch is crazy, JoJo. She'll get both of you killed.

Sage: IT'S NOT WHAT YOU THINK.

"You have to stop." I swivel my whole body toward Trish.

"Like hell I will!" she exclaims with an evil laugh. Dude. Okay. Trish might be a little on the psychotic side. Plus, she is plucking out another cigarette from her magical, never-ending pack. I grab her shoulder and squeeze lightly so she doesn't do something reckless in an attempt to gain her full attention.

"Trish, you're spinning. Stop the car or I'll take all your tips," I threaten, and the car pulls over so fast my head is swimming again. We're on the shoulder of the highway, in the pitch-black, and Trish leans over my body, throws my door open, and points outside.

"Get the hell outta my car, girl. If you're taking this cheating bastard back, I don't want to hang out with you no more."

That escalated quickly. I grab my stuff and hop out, Sage already pulling behind her with his truck. No matter what happened between him and me, I still trust him more to get me home safe. Wherever home may be. He gets out of his truck and walks toward me, chest puffed up, eyes ablaze, just when Trish hits the gas pedal again and leaves us in a thick cloud of exhaust smoke. We're standing one in front of another. I don't say a thing. Neither does he.

He pulls his phone from his pocket and texts me. I stare at him like he's an absolute lunatic.

Sage: If we talk about it right now, we'll fight again. Come home with me and I'll explain everything.

I don't budge. I don't want to cry. I don't want to fight. But I don't want to be a doormat, either. He's got plenty of girls who'd be happy to play that role for him. But not me. He sighs, texting me again.

Sage: OUR home, JoJo. Don't throw away all these years for a misunderstanding. Pls?

The drive back is soul crushing, no less. The silence hangs in the air like a stench. When we get to the apartment, I kick my Chucks against the wall and walk over to my room. A big hand grabs me by the waist and spins me around. I swat it away, feeling all the humiliation, anger, and sadness I'd felt at Barnie's returning, burning in me like a red-hot wrath.

"What the hell, Sage. Get off me! All this bull-shit about me being in your blood didn't feel so true when you ran after Amber, begging."

"You are in my blood!" he screams in my face, raking his fingers along his thick, lush blond hair. I look away so he won't see the tears. My cheeks are wet, and my heart is pounding loud enough to hear from across the room. "You're in my blood, in my veins, in my fucking soul. You're in my heart and in my fingertips and on my fucking lips like a prayer. You're fucking *everywhere,* Jolie Louis. Always will be." He pushes me to the wall. My back slams against it. I growl, pushing him away. He lets me. We're angry. We're desperate. We're frustrated.

"That Amber chick called me a slut today! And you ran after her! Pleaded for her to stay when you thought I wasn't there!"

"I don't want Amber," he says, his lips pursing and his eyes thinning into slits. "I don't want anyone else. I only want you."

"You have a funny way of showing it," I huff—oh,

God, since when did I become a huffer?—turning my back to him and walking toward the hallway. He pins me against the wall again, this time bracing his arms above my head and locking me in. I can't run. I can't hide. I have to stay here and see this through. His eyes are burning. My body is heaving. There's an impending storm between us and we're both exposed.

"She *just* had a miscarriage," he growls into my face, his breath laced with beer and cinnamon gum. "We hooked up a few months ago. The condom broke. She wanted to keep it, and I couldn't exactly tell her not to. She found out last month, and she is a mess about it. That's why I was running after her. She just found out about us at the library."

I swallow a bitter lump of tears. Oh, my God. Poor Amber. Poor, poor Amber. And poor Sage. I've been so focused on how I feel, I forgot that there were other people around me.

"Sage." I cup his cheeks with my palms, my chin quivering.

"I've never wanted anyone but you, JoJo. Not truly. Not wholly. Not obsessively." He steps closer to me, his body flush against mine, his leg between my thighs, his lips on mine as he speaks these words. "You want the truth? Here's the truth: I asked you to be my fake girlfriend because Mark wanted to make a move on you. And it occurred to me, out

L.J. SHEN

of fucking nowhere, that I'd rather die than see you with someone else who holds the potential to give you the things that you need. It occurred to me that I would never be able to be happy for you if you married someone else. It occurred to me that I can't even think of being with anyone but you, and when I *do* have a child, I want it to be with you. I love you, JoJo. But you already know that. I'm also *in love* with you. Crazy about you. Can't live without you."

I kiss his lips to shut him up and to give him everything he needs, my fingers running through his hair, his hands on my waist, pulling me close. We're one entity. Whole and broken. Happy and sad. Lost and so unbelievably found.

"I love you so much," I breathe, the words pouring from my mouth in a rush. "I've always loved you. From that day in the meadow, when the rain knocked so hard on our bodies I thought we were going to go back home with bruises on our skin. I loved you ever since, and I never stopped loving you. Even when I tried really hard. Even when I dated other men."

He hoists me up, my legs wrapped around his narrow waist, and carries me to his bedroom. Not mine—his. It's a statement. I very rarely wander into his bedroom, and only after I ask and only when I need to take something specific. He lowers me to the bed, ever so carefully, his mouth on mine. Never

13ffg1 fixffal

scg

leaving mine.

He fumbles with his jeans. I fumble with my mini dress. We kiss. We bite. We mess around like the two teenagers who wanted to so bad but never dared. I'm here. All of me. Every single part of me is in the present, and it's raw and beautiful and everything I've ever dreamed about wrapped in a bow made of memories and sweet childhood moments. We strip down in silence, our eyes never leaving one another. We kick our clothes to the foot of the bed and his groin is on mine and our lips are kissing, biting, and caressing. My breasts pop free from my bra, and he takes one of my nipples into his mouth, closing his warm lips over it and circling the areola with his tongue. I arch my back.

"I love you." His breath tickles my sensitive nipple, and he works his way down my torso, peppering feathery, wet, hot kisses all over my shivering body. "I love you, I love you, I fucking love you. No matter what happens in my life, you're the constant thing I can count on. The shelter in the storm, the calm in my chaos."

He bites my inner thigh, and I roll my head onto his pillow that smells of cinnamon and aftershave and *him*. His tongue meets my sensitive flesh, licking my arousal, but this time he is not demanding and starving. He is sweet and considerate.

"Jesus, Sage. *Jesus.*"

I can barely breathe. He is teasing me with his mouth to a point of tears before he slides a finger into me, curling it when he is deep enough to reach my magic spot.

"I love you." He continues kissing my pussy. "And I love you, too, JoJo," he says, and I laugh, swatting his head softly. My orgasm washes through me like an oasis. I shudder quietly before his corded, muscled body rises up and his lips meet mine again for a deep kiss.

"Love you. Have I said that lately?" He nuzzles into the crook of my neck, and I'm in heaven, I'm sure of it. I might even murder the person who wakes me up from this dream.

"Not lately." I kiss his temple. "Better tell me again."

"I love you, Jolie Louis. The kind of love that burns through the skin."

Hmm. Is it bad that I want to tattoo this on my forehead?

We kiss some more while my hand trails down the dusty line of hair arrowing from his belly button to his cock. I fist it and move my hand back and forth. I could do this all day without getting bored. Admiring his body. Learning what gives him pleasure. After a few minutes, he raises his head and looks me in the eye.

"Not to sound dramatic, but, baby, I think I'll die

if I don't fuck you right this minute."

"So do it." I smile. He reaches across his bed and fumbles for a condom in his dresser's drawer. Then he rolls it down his cock as we both watch in awe, as if this is the first time for both of us—and in some weird, screwed-up way, it kind of *is*, at least for me. I'm not a virgin, but I feel like one right now, as he slides on top of me again.

"I love you." It's my turn to say. "Every part of you. The broken boy. The strong man. The light-hearted jock and the heavyhearted kid. Every piece of you is loved and cherished, Sage Poirier. Always remember that."

He enters me in one smooth stroke, and I moan at the sudden sensation of being so full, not only physically, but also mentally. My back curls against the sheet when he starts moving in and out in a rhythm I've yet to experience with a man. His movements have no start nor ending. His hips roll back and forth constantly, like an erotic dance between two bodies, and we quickly find the pace that makes us both pant harder and faster. I've never looked in a man's eyes when we had sex before. It felt too weird. Too awkward. But with Sage, I can't help not to.

His eyes are an open wound.

Mine are a bandage that wants to make it all better for him.

This is it. This is everything I wanted. He and I.

Fully and completely committed to one another. His movements become jerky. I begin to quiver again. I swear I've come with this man more times than I did with all my previous partners combined, which really says a lot about his dedication, but also about men in the sack in general.

"I'm about to come, baby. Please come with me."

I nod. Coming on command is the kind of thing that always made me snicker when I read it in books, but now I get it. It is doable when the person asking you to is the biggest turn-on you know.

We come in each other's arms, with him moaning my name and me whimpering when his cock drills into me one last time, and part ways on a kiss. Both our bodies are covered in sweat. We look spent, happy, and so much younger than our years.

He rolls on his back and stares at the ceiling.

I roll to my side and put a hand on his abs.

"Shit," is all he says. I throw my arm over my eyes and laugh. He's been talking sweet to me for an hour, so it only makes sense he'll be back to his old self now.

"That bad, huh?" I joke. He turns to me and pulls my arm from my face.

"That *good*. I never thought it could feel like this."

"Like what?"

He takes my wrist and presses it against his pouty, perfect lips. "Like forever."

Chapter
EIGHT

Sage

The dirty beige hallways don't feel quite the same the day after.

Neither does the cafeteria, which constantly smells of stale pretzels and burnt coffee.

Neither does my body. Nope. It feels lighter and much more capable.

And if I were anyone else, I'd probably say some bullshit about being a different man, but unfortunately for the world, I'm still the same douchy jock. The only difference is I now have sex with my best friend (six times in less than twenty-four hours, but who is counting?), and I don't want to read too much into this, but damn, it puts a stupid-ass smile on my face, which I can't seem to wipe off.

Enter: Amber.

I see her coming out of Sabatta Hall just as I

make my way to the weight room. I stop. Last night, we left everything hanging, and as much as I felt bad about her miscarriage—the doctor told her it might've been due to the fact that she still drank heavily at parties before she'd found out about the pregnancy—I was too fucking wrapped in my own universe with JoJo. Which is shitty, I know. So I stop and clap a hand over her shoulder. She looks tired, and I feel guilty. When Amber found out that she was pregnant, I said I'd support her no matter what. She wanted to keep it, but still hadn't told her parents. Then the miscarriage happened three weeks ago and I've been trying to be there for her, but most of the time, that entails her telling me we need to try to have a baby again.

"Yo. What's up?" I squeeze her shoulder softly, giving her my most genuine smile. People pass us by, talking to each other, laughing. Amber shoots me a look, flipping her blonde, straight hair on an eye roll.

"What do you want, Poirier?" Her voice is pointed, like her expression. I look left and right, somehow still freaked out about JoJo seeing us. Even though I know she gets it. She's the kindest girl I've ever met. She felt so guilty about what happened to Amber. Like she had something to do with it somehow.

"To check how you're doing." I ignore her snark.

"See if you need anything."

"I need you to stop fucking around and give me attention. That's what I need." She juts her chin out, defying me. I scratch the back of my neck, trying to figure out if this is a joke. Throughout the last month, I've been her designated bitch. Drove her places. Let her hang out with the boys and me at Barnie's. Even helped her with her studies. She tried to hit on me countless times, and I blocked it, because even though we shared a fling, I really couldn't see us doing anything more. So this is unwarranted at best and rude at worst.

"Huh?" I cock my head sideways. She slaps my chest. Hard. I take a step back, looking at her like she drank from the crazy fountain, then ate a big dish of psycho.

"You," she points at me, her eyes narrowing, "are not focused on what's important. I just lost our child, Poirier. Do you get what I'm saying? I'm mourning. I'm hurt. I don't need to see you parading your new piece all over campus, telling people she's your girlfriend. It's *so* disrespectful."

What. The. Fuck.

I straighten my back, shaking off some of my surprise.

"I really have no idea what in the good fuck you're talking about, woman. Jolie is not a piece. She's my childhood friend and we're dating now. It has nothing to do with me wanting to be there for you. When we hooked up, I said it was for fun. We had fun. The condom broke. Not so fun. Shit happened in-between. Fucking terrible, I know. Now we're dealing with this. Together. Look, I'm still here for you, yeah? But this has nothing to do with JoJo."

Her lower lip is shaking. People are starting to stop and look. Stall with their phones. Pretend to mess around with their bags. Shit. It's becoming a scene, and that's a problem. I take Amber by the elbow and usher her outside, away from the hall and toward a tree overlooking the entrance of the building. It's a gray day, and no one is out but us. I lean over her—not too close to give her the wrong idea, but close enough so that she knows that I'm serious.

"Anything you need," I say, "I'm here for you. I mean it."

"I need you to leave her." Amber's tears are now falling like a flood, and I want to stop them, I do, but I can't. Not the way she wants me to.

"Amber…"

She throws herself at me, her fists curling around the collar of my jersey. She gets into my face. "Please, Sage. Give us a chance. You're going away next year. Do you think Jolie will go with you? She's not the kind of girl to leave her family. I know her type. I'll do it for you, Sage. I'll leave this place for you."

My eyes darken, and my thoughts jumble in my head. So when Amber seeks my warmth, burrowing into me for a hug, I give it to her.

Because I gave her something else without meaning to.

And now she lost it.

Because I need to make this right for her somehow.

And because I'm afraid that she is right about JoJo.

Jolie

You know the part in the movie where the couple gets together and everything works out and everyone gets their happy ending? Well, this is *not* what happens in real life. At least not to me.

The day starts with Chelsea informing me that she and Mark are not going to the Christmas charity event in New York because she has a job interview for an au pair position in Canada. The woman is heavily pregnant and looking for a full-time nanny to assist her when the baby is born. Mark is going with her, and they'll be flying back to spend

Christmas with her family right after. They're moving fast, and I'm happy for them, but at the same time, I wanted so badly to spend time with my best friend in the Big Apple.

Then, I get fired by a text message. Travis, my boss, who apparently has the diplomatic skills of a swordfish, sends me the following message:

Hi, Julie. Trish told me you had a falling out yesterday. I'm going to be completely honest. She's been with us for a decade now and this could be a problem. I think it's best for everyone if you just hand in your resignation tomorrow after your shift. Thanks for your service and stuff. – Trav.

At first, I think about firing him back my unfiltered response:

Hi, Gravis (oh? You're not Gravis? Well, guess what, I'm not Julie. It's Jolie, you prick!). No need to sugarcoat it. You want me gone because you and Trish meet at the kitchen three times a week before her shift and do some ungodly (and unsanitary) things on the counter. I am more than happy to offer my excellent services to someone who appreciates them. Have a nice life. –Jolie.

But, of course, like the good Southern girl that I

am, I settle for being agreeable:

> *Travis, thank you for your message. I regret to hear about your firing me (because that's essentially what this is), but I'm in no way going to argue with you about it. Since your response to my altercation with Trish was immediate, I think it is only fair that my resignation will be immediate, as well. I will drop by to pick up my last check next week at a time of your convenience. Thanks.*
> *–Jolie.*

After getting fired—just when I think things cannot get any possibly worse—I land my butt in a library's chair, trying to study for my next lit exam, and open up my MacBook. Five seconds into reading an essay about the history of the English language, I rub my eyes, trying to concentrate. When I feel something gooey and warm connecting with the side of my head, I freeze. It slithers down my hair and slaps my face, and my first reaction is to cover my face with both palms. After I hear the knock of whatever's been thrown at me dropping to the floor, I raise my head and look to my right, where the thing came from.

Amber.

Sitting at the desk beside me.

Smiling.

I look down. It's a Starbucks cup. I touch my hair, sniff around me, the shock still working its way to my system. It's my now-cold pumpkin latte with marshmallow. Jesus H.

Bitch.

I know her reasoning behind it, and I get it, I do—it hurts. I can't even begin to imagine how much. But it is also not my fault.

My chair scrapes the floor as I stand up and make my way to her. She is sitting with her sorority friends, their army of cardigans, pearl necklaces, and mechanically straightened hair in full attendance. I look sloppy in comparison. My Chucks are dirty, my blonde is also red, and my clothes are too casual. And still, they can't treat me this way. Ever.

"You need to stop this." I slap my hand on her desk, lifting my chin up to look down at her. She stares up at me with a conceited smile I'm dying to wipe off of her face.

"No, I don't. You have something of mine that I want back."

"And I suppose that'd be Sage?" I tilt my head sideways. She shrugs, snorting out an unattractive laugh she'd never allow herself in his presence.

"And his money. And his future. And his status. Basically, everything. The best thing about being upfront with you about it, is that you're too goody-two-shoes to even tell him I ever said it. Because you don't talk badly of people, do you, sweet girl? I know all about you and your running-to-see-mommy-every-other-weekend tactics."

Tactics?

Tactics?!

She thinks I go through life trying to impress someone? My best friend? Is she nuts? I don't even need anyone to answer this question. Of course, she's nuts. No one of sound mind would ever think in this direction. I lower my body, lean into her face, and whisper, "I know what happened to you, and I'm sorry that it did. I am. But you cannot break us up, Amber. I suggest you move on, and while you're at it, take a very long look at your behavior and priorities. Because you're not being assertive or streetsmart here, girl. You're being a manipulative bitch."

The words slap her, one by one, and I see her cocky smile melting into a shocked, wide-eyed grimace. One of her friends—a brunette who is wearing a lemon yellow cardigan and a matching headband—crinkles her nose.

"Wait, how do you mean after what happened to you? What exactly happened to you?"

"I...I..."

Another girl, who sits directly in front of her, bolts up from her chair and shakes her head. Her face is so red it is completely possible she might explode.

"Jesus Christ, Amber! Tell me you didn't go through with that stupid plan! Faking a pregnancy and then a miscarriage? Like, hello, newsflash! Your life is not a bad *General Hospital* episode!"

I stagger backwards, gripping the end of my desk and staring at a very embarrassed, very angry Amber as her eyes broaden and her chest heaves up and down, the adrenaline of the lie catching up with reality.

Everything turns red.

Then black.

Then white again, because the lie is not mine. Not mine to keep, to be burdened with, nor to carry.

I turn around to collect my MacBook and my shoulder bag and dash outside the library door, making my way to the nearest bus station back home. Amber is after me. I hear her heels clacking against the floor. I don't turn around, mainly because the notion that I can do something terrible to her—slap her, yell at her, or curse her out—is strong.

She might be that kind of person, but I'm not.

Just as I round the corner of the street, Chelsea's blue Buick appears from the intersection. She stops in front of me with a screech and throws the passenger's door open.

"Need a getaway ride?"

"That seems to be the reoccurring theme in my life right now."

I hop in, then I watch Amber's disappearing figure through the side mirror as my heart finally returns to its usual rhythm.

"More coffee stains?" Chelsea chuckles, her eyes scanning my blouse. I smile, avoiding the full story.

"That's right. I'm starting to believe they're my sign for good luck."

Chapter
NINE

Sage

Four days before Christmas Eve.

"You ready?" I ask, staring at the mirror as I fasten my cufflinks. The crisp dress shirt is a Prada, and it's weird to wear Prada. It's weird to be able to *afford* Prada, and I constantly have to remind myself that this is a one-off. I bought this suit for the meeting I had with the Raiders in California because JoJo made me. She said I needed to dress the way I wanted to feel. Well, today I feel like I'm going to fulfill my dream and become a professional football player as of next spring.

That's one of two dreams down, one more to go.

"Just a sec!" my girl calls out from the bathroom at the fancy hotel room. Even though I've known her ever since we were kids, there is a lot I'm finding out about her, now that we're dating. Like how it takes her literally two hours to get ready to go out, even though she doesn't need more than two minutes to get ready for school when we leave for campus every morning, or that she is really (ironically) horny when she's on her period, which makes us hella creative in bed (I don't mind a little blood on my sword), but she does. Or that she is not actually that sensitive or sweet when she has a reason not to be—like that time she came back home and told me how Amber goddamn tricked me into babying her. I still haven't recovered from that shit.

Wait, that's not true. I totally did. But still. What an asshole that girl is.

"Okay! Close your eyes," she says. My tie is still loose around my neck, and I frown, turn around, lean a hip against the dresser, and shove my hands into my pockets.

"All right. Let's see it."

"That's the whole point, Sage! You can't see it! Eyes closed, remember?" she squeaks. *Squeaks*. I make her squeak these days. I never did that when we were friends. She also does a lot of huffing, especially when I ask her if we can have sex in insane places like the plane or the beach. I think she huffs to let me know that the idea *is* insane, but we still end up doing it all the same.

"Yeah, yeah, eyes as closed as your legs this evening," I mutter, squeezing my eyelids together.

"That's right, mister. No Christmas quickie in the bathroom."

I hear her voice getting closer, and my cock jerks in appreciation. He always liked pretty things, and she is gorgeous eye candy. My girl, with the Chucks and the strawberry blonde hair who is not afraid to run in the rain for me.

"I'd like to negotiate this part." I lick my lips, my eyes still closed. I feel her closer. Her heat. Her body. The clack of her heels, which I've yet to see.

"I'm sorry. I do not negotiate with terrorists."

I smirk. "Oh, we'll see about that by the end of the night."

"Open," she says, close enough to me that I can smell her flowery perfume, but not so close that I can feel her breath on my skin. I open my eyes, and she is standing there in a long red dress with a deep slit that exposes a shapely, milky leg. The dress is all velvet, prompting me to want to touch it. To tear it. To fucking eat her out on the floor. But I still want my balls intact when we get to the gala at the Met. She's wearing minimal makeup—other than her red-hot lips—and a pair of heels where the soles are red. The expensive stuff. What I urged her to buy when I signed the deal with the Raiders, same day I got my suit. Her scarlet lips twitch into a timid smile.

"What do you think?"

"I think you look perfect, but there's one thing that's missing. Accessories. Turn around."

Her eyes widen, but she does as I ask. She turns around, and I open the drawer behind me and produce my gifts for her. I pull her hair up to put her necklace on. Nothing too fancy. A pink gold necklace with one lonely pearl. It takes me a few seconds to fasten it—this is not the movies. It's real life, and my hands are shaking like a motherfucker.

"Now back to me," I say. My voice breaks. She turns around. Slowly. So slowly. Super slowly. Why is she so slow? Is this a sign? *Shut up, asshole. Just do it.*

Very nonchalantly, like it's not a big deal, like I'm not shitting myself, I slide the ring onto her engagement finger. Like the necklace, it is simple and elegant. Thin, with one diamond sparkling in the middle. Lonely and rare, just like my girl.

I don't ask; I state.

Jolie Louis' heart belongs to me. It will always belong to me. It belonged to me the minute she decided to open her rusty window and sneak out of her room to meet me, uninvited, but all the same needed.

She looks down at the ring, and I expect her to frown, maybe ask a question, but no. She doesn't do any of those things. She looks back up, smiles, and uses her newly adorned left hand to cup my face and pull me close.

Outside, a storm is making the newspapers and trash on the streets of New York dance in circles. Inside, it's warm. We kiss. Like friends. Like lovers. Like everything in-between.

"I love you, angry boy," she says, and I answer her with the only thing that pops into my head.

"I love you, brave girl."

Epilogue

One Year Later

On the eighth beat of silence, she finally opened her mouth.

It was dry, and numb, and painful from smiling all day, but she wanted to utter these words, even if they were the last she'd ever say.

"I, Jolie Alexandra Louis, take you, Sage Albert Poirier, to be my best friend, my faithful partner, and my one true love. You'll be my storm in the summer, my calm under the winter sky, and all the seasons in-between. To have, to hold, to cherish, and to comfort." She slid the ring with shaky fingers, their childhood tree standing in the background, wrapped in red and white sateen bows. It was a small ceremony, with only their beloved family members and college friends as witnesses. No matter how much of a superstar the boy grew up to be in his career with the Raiders, they were still the same kids from twelve years ago. Humble. Quiet. In love. *In love.* So, so in love.

"You may now kiss the bride," the priest said, his words trickling down the two lovers' souls, melting like the wedding cake behind them on that hot summer day.

On the eighth second after the girl vowed to give her all to the boy, the boy smirked and said, "Don't have to tell me twice, sir." He pulled the veil off of her face, cupped her cheeks, and kissed her so hard he stole her breath away.

People bolted up from their seats, cheering, whistling, laughing, and *living in* the moment. The girl smiled, reminiscing back to the very first time she summoned the courage to follow the broken boy, to follow her instincts, to follow her heart, and to talk to him.

Their lips moved together in a dance of love and lust. They knew the moves by heart.

On the eighth minute after the ceremony was over, the girl sauntered across the carefully cut grass to her best friend, Chelsea, putting her hand on her shoulder. Chelsea turned around, her date—Mark, whom she was now engaged to—decided to make himself scarce, muttering his congratulations as he walked away. Sage appeared by his new bride's side, his smile so big, it hit both women like a sunray.

"What's up?" Chelsea asked. She'd recently moved from Vancouver—where she lived with her fiancé—back to Louisiana, where they were both looking for jobs, eager to settle down.

"What's your schedule like in eight months?" the girl inquired, butterflies taking flight in her stomach. Chelsea lifted one eyebrow. Sage was on the verge of exploding from happiness. The girl moved her open palm across her white dress, sliding down her flat stomach.

"Pretty clear. Why?" Chelsea probed.

"Because you're hired," the girl said, as all three sets of eyes drifted down to her abdomen.

The girl got a kiss on the lips from the boy who no longer howled at the moon and cried on a tree. On the forehead. Like friends do.

Then he kissed her on the lips, like lovers do.

Then he kissed the inside of her wrists, like soulmates do.

The END (ZONE)

Acknowledgements

This year has been an incredible journey for me. My readers, fellow authors, agent, editors, and friends took me places I never thought I'd reach. So much so, in fact, that I didn't want to end this year without giving my readers a treat.

The End Zone was never supposed to happen. I don't usually write novellas. I love evoking my readers' different feelings and there's nothing I enjoy more than slow-burn romances. At the same time, I felt like I needed to give you something sweet and cute for the holidays, and I hope I did just that.

I would like to thank the following people from the bottom of my heart:

My beta readers, Tijuana Turner, Mia Sparks, Lana Kart, and Paige Jennifer. Thank you so much for putting up with my crazy schedule and for your attention for detail. You make my books so, so much better.

To my editors, Paige Smith and Tamara Mataya. I love our journey together. Your advice and guidance are everything an author could wish for and more. I am constantly honing my craft and you push me to my limits as I grow as an artist.

To Letitia Hasser. Please don't hate me. I know I don't know what I want half the time, but if it makes you feel any better, you have to put up with it a few times a year. My husband needs to tolerate it three-four times a week at a restaurant or when we choose furniture! Imagine that.

To my unicorn team—my amazing agent Kimberly Brower at Brower Literary, Sunny Borek, Ella Fox, Ava Harrison, my street team, and my formatter Stacey Ryan Blake. Thank you for being true professionals through and through. I am so, so lucky to have you.

To the Sassy Sparrows—I love you! Thank you for brightening my day, every single day. Going through this journey with you is such a blessing.

Last but not least—dear readers, thank you so much for making me what I am today. An author, an artist, and against all odds, someone who can stay at home and write for a living. I do not take that lightly. I will not let you down. There's so much more to come, and I'm excited for all of it.

I'm leaving you with a treat I've been wanting to share with you for so long—the first chapter of my next full-length, standalone, *Midnight Blue*. This novel has put me through the ringer and I cannot wait to give it to you. Hope you enjoy!

Thank you,
L.J. Shen xoxo

The
END
ZONE

Extended Epilogue

Jolie

"**M**ommy, can I have a cock?" My three-year-old daughter is staring at me with the intensity of a drama major, all big, crayon green eyes and molten gold locks like her father. I spray my coffee evenly between the morning newspaper, the iPad Sage got me last Christmas, and my usual uniform of yoga pants and flirty tank top.

"Excuse me?" I narrow my eyes at my little baby. *My. Little. Baby. Let those words sink, Jolie.* Who taught her that word? I think I'm going to throw up.

"Yusss." Elle hops up on the chair beside me at the breakfast table, making a show of spreading her arms wide before hugging an invisible *cock* to her chest. Okay. Now I'm definitely going to throw up. Side note: my child is very optimistic as to the size of cocks.

"My friend Staci has one." She clutches the invisible cock to her chest, nuzzling her nose against it.

"Your friend Staci has a cock?"

Elle nods. "And the cock has a wife. And soon they'll have little, baby cocks."

"Oh. *Ohhh*. You mean that kind of cock." My heart rate slows back to beats that don't threaten to smash through my ribcage. I'm kind of embarrassed my mind drifted automatically to *that* place. Then again, I've been hornier than a unicorn recently. I pat my cheeks with my palms to cool them down and stand up to grab a dishtowel to clean the mess I've made.

"What other kind of cock is there?"

One day you'll know, my child. But hopefully not before thirty.

"I want all the cocks in the world. The mommy, the daddy, the kids…"

"That could be arranged, if you'd only be so kind as to use another name for the family," I mutter absentmindedly as I wipe off the fresh stains of coffee on the table. I tell Elle to go pick a pair of shoes ahead of her school day. I know it's a task that will take her ten to fifteen minutes at the very least. Girl is Oscar-ready every time she sets foot in that pre-school.

From that point on, I do everything on au-to-pilot. Clean the breakfast table. Wash the dishes. Water the plants. Dump food inside Rebel's bowl (he is our Yorkshire terrier, no need to call CPS). I bend down to pick up a stray Cheerio Elle must've tried to slam-dunk into Rebel's bowl, when my world stops spinning on its axis and hangs over an abyss of darkness.

The first word going through my mind is *no*.

Followed by: *Oh, hell no.*

The panic dribbles into my bloodstream in drops at first. *Drip, drip, drip.* But the trickle soon becomes a stream, and the terror turns to anger as I snatch the small thing from under Sage's usual chair and stand up, feeling dizzy.

A lipstick.

A lipstick that's not mine.

The shade too red, too hot, too sexy for yours truly to actually consider buying. I wear neutral colored lip glosses in flirty shades with names like "Summer Rivers" and "Spring Break". This is a full-blown Marilyn Monroe lipstick. What the hell is it doing here?

It's tempting me to spear a steak knife into my husband's chest. That's what it's doing.

I decide the best course of action is not, in fact, to call him during his training camp in Colorado and yell at him until every vocal cord in my throat tears apart. It is very early in the morning in California, but I know my mama in Louisiana is already up and going about her day. I dial her number, turning my back on Elle's room so she won't see her mommy crying. The tears are skating down my cheeks in fat, salty drops.

How could he do this to me?

Childhood friends. College sweethearts. Undeniable soulmates. Since we got together four years ago, we've been nothing but lovey-dovey. Call me a fool, but I never thought he'd cheat on me. It always seemed like he only had eyes for me.

I moved to California for him.

I said goodbye to my family for him.

I turned my back on my dream to become a teacher so he could focus on his career.

All.

For.

Him.

"Hello? Honey pie?" Mama chirps and, just like that, my chest crumbles as I heave out a sob.

"Sage is cheating on me," the words tumble from my mouth, and I let all the anger and panic building inside me loose. It's like a river now, no longer coming in trickling drips and drops. I'm mentally rummaging through the catalog of women we have coming into our house on a regular basis as I clutch the lipstick like a weapon. I have friends. Lots of them, actually. I invite them here frequently. But none of them wear a red lipstick. We usually chill in our Lululemons during playdates, drink wine, and try to keep all the children in one piece. Think less The Duchess of Cambridge and more Cameron Diaz leaving Equinox. Still cute, but in a non-threatening way.

"Jolie…" Mama trails off, a mixture of shock and warning in her voice. "No, honey. There is just no way."

"There is, apparently. I found a stranger's lipstick in my house. So tacky."

"Mommy?" Elle is standing at the door, holding onto her Hello Kitty rain jacket, with the ears on the hoodie and everything. "Why are you sad?"

I wipe my eyes hurriedly, mentally maiming myself for not holding myself together longer, until I dropped her off. "I'm not sad, baby. I'm happy. We're going to get you a chicken family." I haven't discussed it with Sage yet, but screw Sage. "Now let's get you into that jacket."

"Jolie?" Mama barks from the other line. *Great.* "Jolie? I need to know what is happening right now!"

But it's too late. I mumble a brief goodbye and tuck my phone into my back pocket. I help Elle into her jacket and drive her to school, where I don't know how, but I manage to sit through a thorough examination of a Barbie doll's anatomy, as conducted by Elle and her friend Staci. Let's just say both girls' futures as OB/GYNs is secured, in case their masterplan to become astronaut ballerinas doesn't pan out.

Once I step out of my daughter's class, my phone begins buzzing in my pocket. I pluck it out.

Sage.

I want to take the call and tell him that he is a bastard of the highest degree, but instead, I let the call die. I need to collect my scattered thoughts before I hear him out. I'm too angry and confused. One moment I think it is all done and dusted, and our marriage is over, and the other, I inwardly laugh at myself for jumping to such an idiotic conclusion.

And so, I plan to deal with this matter in the same fashion every grown-up woman does—I am going to get shitfaced at home and wait for the problem to solve itself.

On my way back home (screw yoga. Apparently, life happens when you Shavasana for eight straight minutes in a boiling hot room), I kill three more attempts by Sage to call me. Two more by Mama. It is obvious there is a correlation between the two. She told him. Good. I know it's only a matter of time until the text messages start pouring in. Of course, there may be a plausible explanation for the lipstick.

But the thing is, for some reason that is beyond me right now, I *want* to be mad. And angry. And unreasonable. Another thing I want: ice cream. No. I *need* ice cream. Like a flower needs the sun and Taylor Swift needs to stop dating douchebags. The urge is *real*.

Sage is quick to deliver on the text messages front.

Sage: I can explain.

Sage: But not right now. You'll have to wait a few weeks.

Sage: You'll need to trust me on this one.

Sage: You really think I'm cheating on you? Are you high or something? Have you been asleep the past DECADE?

Sage: I hope you weren't upset in front of Elle.

Sage: Answer me.

Sage: I'm coming back home, and my coach and manager are not going to be happy about it.

Sage: There'll be a lot of ass-kissing afterwards. We'll have to entertain them AND their wives to smooth things over. But you asked for it.

Sage: You better be naked when I get there. I'm taking the next flight home.

Sage: At the airport now. So. You think I'm cheating on you. Do you also think I'm brain-dead by any chance? Why the hell would I cheat on you in our house? I can afford a nice hotel room.

Sage: Although I'm guessing that's not what you want to hear...

I'm holding my first glass of wine. It looks good in my hand. You know what else looks good? A cheeseburger. I decide to neglect the wine, pick up my phone and Uber-eat it. Life is too short to pick up your own food. Especially when your husband may be cheating on you. I call Elle's babysitter, because there is no way I'm picking her up from preschool piss drunk. "I need you to take Elle for a few hours after school."

"Count on it."

The hours tick by. The cheeseburger is consumed, digested, and reminds me why raw onion is the work of Satan. I'm currently watching *Friends*. If Jennifer Aniston bounced back after *Brangelina*, this, too, shall pass. Right?

Wrong. I feel like throwing myself off a cliff.

The only thing stopping me is Elle.

But somewhere deep down, even though my husband is offering me zero explanation for the lipstick, I'm still not convinced Sage has cheated. I just feel...angry. And sad. And happy. And horny.

Jesus Lord, what is happening to me?

I stand up to get myself another bottle of wine when the door opens.

I'm not expecting anyone.

I look up at the overhead clock. Jesus, it's already

the afternoon.

I swivel my head back toward the door.

My husband is standing there, looking just about ready to murder someone.

Someone unreasonable.

Someone hormonal.

Someone like me.

Sage

Sometimes dicking your wife is not a matter of want. You need to do it as a national service.

Like, when she starts to have random, weird, unhealthy thoughts that are completely unwarranted. I can't tell her who the lipstick belongs to, because it's part of a surprise. A surprise I'm hoping will result in a lot of anal. Not—in fact—a divorce.

"What the fuck, JoJo?" I drop my duffel on the floor and advance on her. We are twenty-five now. Older and wiser than we were when our one-time roomie hookup took place. She should know better than to think I'd bang some random, and in our house, of all places. Jesus Christ, who does she think I am?

Sage Poirier. The guy who banged his way through every girl in college. What else should she think?

JoJo does what she always does when she knows I am going to catch her—she runs. This time, she darts to the bathroom, slapping the wall as she rounds the corner. Big mistake. I was thinking about bathroom sex all throughout my speedy flight from Colorado. She gallops to the en-suite in our room, and I'm on her heels, faster and stronger and with the instincts of a pro athlete. I wasn't drafted to one of the most popular teams in the NFL for nothing.

"Not so fast, little rascal." I hook my arm around her waist and jerk her into my raging erection. I've been thinking about that sad, sulky face of hers the entire flight back home. I'm going to get so much shit from my coach and manager for bailing on my team, and this is so out of character from my sensible, reasonable, not to mention *sane* wife. The least I deserve is a sex worthy of my trouble.

"What are you doing?" she hisses, baring her teeth.

"What the fuck does it look like?" I grind my cock into her ass and the friction alone could start a fire. Goddamn JoJo and her love for yoga. Her body is lithe and tight everywhere, yet her skin is the softest thing I've ever touched. It's like I was born to be weak for her, and only her. No one else but her. "I'm baking a cake. Nope. Wait. I'm claiming what's mine.

And it just so happens to be a very mouthy, very impulsive wife who thinks very little of me." I flatten my palm on her lower back and bend her over our Jack and Jill sink in one swift movement. Our eyes meet in the mirror. Jolie is panting hard, her body quivering under my big palm, shaking, *anticipating*. I'm not sure if she is more angry or turned on. Doesn't matter. Either will get her to come so hard she'll turn into Jell-O.

"You think I'm cheating on you?" I ask, my voice low, never breaking our gaze.

"I think I never wear red lipstick. Nor do any of my friends." Her eyes narrow at the mirror defiantly, but she is pushing her ass into me, and I dig my fingers into her delicate flesh under her clothes, probably marring it red.

I push her yoga pants down, then get rid of her tiny white thong. I would tear it off of her and leave marks on her ass if it wasn't for the fact I'm truly fond of these panties. "Listen to me carefully, *Wifey*," I spit up the title with enough venom to show her that she wasn't the only person to get butthurt today. "No matter what you think you've seen or caught me doing, even if it looks so bad you want to pluck my eyeballs, rest assured, there's a good explanation for it. I will never cheat on you. I will never look at another woman. I barely even register other women exist, save for my mama and Elle."

My dick springs free from my briefs the minute I shove my jeans down, pressing it into her pussy, that's already swollen and dripping with her want for me. I poke at her slit, so pink and wet and ready for me, torturing her like she tortured me when she chose not to answer any of my messages and calls.

"You like that?" I breathe into her ear and her entire body blossoms into goosebumps, melting under my touch like butter under the blistering sun.

"Fuck me," she growls quietly, throwing her head back against my shoulder and squeezing her eyes shut. Yeah. Like hell I will. She will have to beg for it now.

"You want a cheater to fuck you?"

"If you cheated, I want you to get the hell out of my house. But…fuck me first. Jesus." Her head drops to the cold tiles and she closes her eyes, pushing her pussy into my cock. Jesus sounds about right. She hates what comes out of her mouth, but she isn't going to take it back, because it's true. She would give me permission to fuck her right now even if I'd killed Rebel, our dog. I can feel the moisture crawling down her inner thighs. JoJo's always been hot for me.

"Spread your legs," I growl into her ear. She does. I drive into her once, my thrust in sync with her—that's what we do, we are legends inside our bedroom, gods who play a very sinful game—and pull out immediately.

"Ohhh…" She shivers all over, her knees wobbly.

"Oh-in-fucking-deed. Now tell me again. Do you really think I would cheat on the love of my life? Bring a stranger into the home I built with you, to the place where we raise our daughter?"

"I…I…" she stutters.

"Bring me that lipstick. I know you kept it. *Now*."

It takes Jolie a few seconds to compose herself, straighten her posture and stalk out of the bathroom to get the red lipstick. She returns naked from the waist down, a pink camisole hanging loose around her chest. I snatch the lipstick from her hand, pop it open, and *whaddayaknow*, it is brand new. I'm happy the person it belongs to didn't use it yet, or I would get a lot of shit for what I'm about to do.

"Come here," I seethe. She does. When she is close enough to me, I apply the lipstick to her lips, grab her hair, and push her down to her knees.

"I love you, sweetheart, but you were very bad to reach such an incorrect conclusion too fast, too soon, and without giving me the chance to explain myself. You also brought me here all the way from Colorado, so you better suck my dick like a goddamn Hoover, otherwise you're not coming for an entire month."

I've never seen someone so hungry for a dick. She devours my long, thick shaft, the red lipstick smearing all over my skin and her face. A thick drop of cum dangles from my tip, and she hurries to swallow it into her mouth. She is sucking, lapping, slurping, pulling, and my balls are tightening in pleasure and awe. JoJo is really, truly, carnally in love with my dick. Which is a good thing, because I would legitimately marry her pussy if it was legal.

Don't say that out loud. She is acting crazy this week. She might blame you for wanting to cheat on her again.

Most of my cock disappears inside her pretty mouth when I decide, "You don't deserve my cum in your mouth."

I hoist her up to her feet and throw her back against the counter. I bend her over again, push my hand between her thighs and borrow some of her juices. Her greedy pussy is so wet, it is literally dripping, and I rub it all over her skin, then suck my fingers to taste what I do to her. She bucks her hips, begging for my hand, for some friction, for anything, but I curl my fingers to borrow her juices and smear them into her tight back hole.

"You don't deserve my cock," I groan, pushing my cock—wet from the blow job—into her tight little ass. "But you'll get something, JoJo. You've been good to me so far, so I'm going to let you come. As long as you know I won't be so fucking nice the next time you accuse me of cheating."

She nods enthusiastically as I push into her slowly from behind, one hand guiding my cock, the other plucking out the electrical toothbrush by her sink.

"Yes. Oh, God, yes, Sage. I promise. I promise." She is falling apart at my first thrust into her ass. Jolie is a sexual animal, but right now she is borderline possessed. I wonder what she had for lunch and how do I get her to eat it three times a day so we can always do it like rabbits.

"Open your legs wider for me," I bark out the order, watching her beautiful, innocent face smeared with red lipstick as I fuck her ass mercilessly. She does. I press my thumb to the button of the electric toothbrush and it vibrates alive as I shove it into her pussy, filling her ass and cunt at the very same time, and thrusting both holes in the same, punishing rhythm.

"Sage! My Lord, Sage!" she is screaming now. I've never done that before. Taken both her holes. Not entirely possible with only one cock, and that's usually how it goes in the human anatomy. Anal is also a special treat in her marriage, so I'm going to go ahead and guess that my wife is going through something highly hormonal to be acting like this. The vibration from the toothbrush makes her ribcage rattle, and I take the hand that guided my cock into her and pinch her nipple hard.

"You wanna know the worst part?"

She gulps loudly, but doesn't answer me.

"The lipstick was a part of a very good surprise."

"Huh?"

"Oh yeah." I drill harder, deeper, faster into her, feeling her orgasm washing over both of us. The violent tremble of her ass against my body. My dick is pulsing with heat, and I know I'm about to burst, too. "That lipstick, baby, belonged to a real estate agent. I bought your mama and pop a house next to us, so they can help you with Elle and all our future babies. Now that they're retired"—I pull the toothbrush from her pussy, yanking her by the hair and turning her around. I elevate her over the counter and drag my dick along her thighs, marking her with my cum—"more time to help you. And you'll need all the help you can get, honey, because with the amount of fucking we do, we are going to populate the entire state."

She comes so hard, her sweet cunt clutches the fingers I shove into her in a death grip. I almost stumble backwards from the impact of shooting my own load between her thighs, the scent of her juices, our sweat and our sex mingling together in the air like a perfect cocktail. I grab her jaw in my hand and guide her lips to mine, planting an all-consuming kiss to seal this fuck on the right note.

"I love you, Jolie. You're my world, my universe, the air I fucking breathe. I will never cheat on you, and next time you pull a stunt like this, I *will* punish you with unfulfilled orgasms. You better believe it."

With that, I turn around and stalk out of the bathroom, leaving her to collapse on the floor to regroup.

I can feel her gaze on my back.

It tells me I redeemed myself.

That she is in love.

I look down at my deflating cock, tucking it back into my briefs as I turn the shower on for us to share together. As I wait for the water to warm up, I think back to the last time we had such crazy sex. I vaguely remember she was acting weird, too.

I swivel my head back to watch her, and the penny drops.

It was right after we found out Elle was coming for us.

"Baby," I say.

"Yeah?"

"After the shower I'm going to go buy you a pregnancy test."

Two weeks after

Jolie

Boy, do I regret drinking those few sips of wine the day Sage came back from Colorado for me.

"Show it to me again." My husband snatches the ultrasound photos from my hand. Oh, God. If guilt was water, I'd be drowning. No matter that I drank two weeks ago, and my doctor told me that I was perfectly fine, and that it didn't matter—I still feel incredibly guilty. Funny thing is, I am on the pill. I wasn't planning on getting pregnant again anytime soon, but it just happened. I wasn't on antibiotics or anything. But as my OB/GYN said, "There's always that small percentage. And you fell right into it."

We look at the ultrasound photos again. Our baby looks like a bean. Or a peanut. Whoops, now I'm hungry again. Pregnancy really is a magical thing.

"Do you think it's going to be a boy or a girl?" Sage looks up at me, his eyes shimmering with joy.

I smile. "It's fifty-fifty."

"What fifty does your gut tell you? That's where the baby is. It must know."

"A boy," I tell him. He smirks, dragging me to sit on his lap. Elle appears from her room, skating across the shiny floor of our house. She comes to a halt beside us, flips her bangs away, and grins.

"Guess what, Daddy?"

"What, baby?"

"Mommy said I can have a cock."

Sage's face turns from smiling to stunned. He twists his head to me, still talking to our baby girl. "Baby, you will not be getting a cock any time before I'm six feet under."

"Sage." I slap his chest lightly, giggling.

He grins. "She means a chicken, right?"

I nod. "I made the same mistake."

Sage pinches my waist. "That's because you're horn—" I flick his ear, so he catches himself, "horribly imaginative."

"I think so, too. By the way, you know what else you are going to get, baby?" I turn to my sweet, beautiful daughter who looks just like her father.

"What?"

"A brother or sister."

Her mouth falls open, and I can't help but laugh.

She frowns. "But…I'm still getting a cock, too, right?"

Sage and I both laugh, and I bury my nose into my husband's delicious neck. There is only one word floating in my head right now, but it's the only one that matters.

Mine.

Surprise Bonus Content

This year started out on an amazing note for me. I was humbled and excited with all the love you have given *Midnight Blue*, my rock star romance, which came out on January 17th. My readers are much more than just readers. They are my tribe, my home, the people who make me push myself harder with each book. I have therefore decided to treat you to a little extended epilogue from *Vicious* (*Sinners of Saint* #1). If you haven't read the novel yet, please skip this part. If you have, I hope you enjoy.

Thank you for your continued support and passion for the written word. You make the world better. Well…at least mine!

Love,

L.J. xoxo

Extended Epilogue: *Vicious*

Emilia

"Kneel."

There's menace in this voice, and I grew to love the man who carries it like a loaded weapon. Every word is a sharp edge of a knife, sinking into my skin.

Kneel.

Sit.

Open your mouth.

Touch yourself.

Repeat after me: Vicious, I'm yours.

Most married couples fall into a blissful, albeit drowsy domestic routine of laundry, family dinners, and Netflix.

Most married couples are not Vicious and me.

We were different from the beginning. A yin and a yang, fighting over which color took more space, black or pink. We started out as enemies, and I think that, although we are still crazy in love, we will always be rivals on some level. We will always be passionate, and angry, and desperate.

We will always be *us*.

"I'm sorry, I don't take orders from people who aren't my boss," I say coolly, dropping my funky, colorful bag at the door and erasing the distance between us in wide, confident steps. He is standing in front of me, his Armani suit impeccable, his raven hair slicked back, his icicle blue eyes devouring me in ways that make being eaten alive worth it. He scans the length of me, a slight sneer on his face. I'm still me, even so many years later. The tips of my light brown hair are still cherry-blossom pink. The soles of my shoes are yellow, for Christ's sake.

"That could be arranged, if you continue your sass."

"How is that going to work, Vicious? Are you going to re-employ me against my will?" For the past eighteen years, I've been managing my own gallery in L.A. A gallery he bought for me shortly before our engagement. I have a career, an income of my own. Truth is, he gave me a push, but the entire journey to where I am today was made by me, and only me, and he knows it.

He cups my cheek, yanks me by the hem of my funky powder blue blouse with little suns into his body and leans down for a kiss. Our lips brush briefly, promising scattered clothes and ragged breaths, just as the door swings open and our son walks in. He slams the door behind him, his eyes still intently glued to his phone.

Vaughn is a spitting image of his dad. So much so, that sometimes it scares me.

At sixteen, he has the walk, talk, and air of

Vicious when the latter was a senior in high school. Rangy, strong body, thick-fringed blue eyes, skin so fair he looks like he defies the sun, and cheekbones you could use as a sharp weapon. More than anything, he has that uniquely-pissed facial expression that tells you that he just doesn't care.

Not about your problems.

Not about your feelings.

And certainly not about what you think about *him*.

"Are you actively trying to be gross?" Vaughn mutters under his breath, throwing his phone on the silk ottoman by the entrance and kicking his shoes off at the same time. His black, holed shirt strains around the muscles of his back as he tears the gray beanie off his head and shoves it into his holed back pocket. His black skinny jeans are ripped not only at the knees, but also below the ass, hanging loosely by a belt made of tied-up shoelaces. Yes. My son is a millionaire who dressed like he should be begging for his next meal.

Because he simply. Doesn't. Care.

Vaughn ambles past us, toward the kitchen, his eyes hooded with an impending storm.

"Are you actively trying to get your ass grounded and your credit card sent back to where all Black American Express cards go to die?" Vicious raises a sardonic eyebrow, smoothing his suit with his palm and taking a sidestep so my body fully covers his erection. I bite down a giggle. Vaughn throws the fridge door open, takes out leftover roasted sprouts and steak, and gets right to business. He places enough food to choke an elephant on a fork and shoves it into his mouth while the food is still cold, leaning one hip against the dark green granite counter.

Vaughn's eyes are hard on the food as he says, "You're supposed to hate each other or get a divorce like most of the other parents at my school. Get the memo, guys."

"Well, we did that in high school. We did everything backwards. Now is our honeymoon phase." I offer him a breezy smile, hoping I can melt his inhibitions and anger as I do with his dad.

Vaughn swallows the steak without even chewing. "Still. Nothing like a parental PDA to kill a guy's appetite. Get a room."

"We *have* a room." I knot my arms around my husband's neck and plant a tender kiss on his cheek. Secretly, I enjoy seeing my son like this. Defiant, strong, outspoken. Everything Vaughn says is in block letters. Important and not to be ignored. His voice is low and looming, only a few tons lighter than his dad's.

"We have fifteen of them, to be exact, and a snotty-ass son who is more than welcome to migrate out of our house in favor of military school." Vicious is clearly joking, but there is a serious edge to his tone. "Apologize to your mother."

Vaughn carries the empty plastic container, now devoid of food, to the stainless steel trash bin and kicks it open with his foot. He dumps it inside and shuts the door with his hip. He turns around, and I realize that his dark expression makes me wince, and I'm *his mom*. I dread to think how other people feel about him at school.

"So terribly sorry, Mother." He does a little bow, his movements drip sarcasm and disdain.

"Would you like to share what got your panties in such a twist, they now need to be surgically removed from your ass?" Vicious flicks his cold eyes from my breasts to his son, finally stepping from behind me. He is no longer suffering from a steel-hard erection. Despite the unfortunate current situation, my husband and my son are close. In fact, they can sit in the media room for hours, talking, playing God of War, and drinking root beer. They share not only blood and family, but also several interests and a weird, tongue-in-cheek sense of humor only they understand. They also share the same scorn toward life and people. They both love the Raiders, and pissing people off, and *me*.

Vaughn swivels on his heel, stalking toward the stairs. Vicious clasps his arm on instinct, pulling him toward us. Their gazes lock and something *clicks* in the air. Whatever passes between them makes goosebumps chase each other up my arms. I've seen Vaughn's expression on Vicious' face before. He gave it to Dean, one of his best friends, shortly before we started dating as teenagers.

"What's wrong?" my husband presses.

Vaughn shakes his touch off, taking a step toward the spiral bare concrete staircase, complete with glass bannisters that give our entire house a modern, raw look. "Nothing."

Vicious captures his arm again, this time tugging him into a fatherly half-hug.

"We don't keep shit from each other in this family, V."

"Yup." Vaughn's head hangs down as a bitter chuckle leaves his lips, so lively red in contrast to his pale skin. He takes a step back from Vicious, and this is strange, because usually, he is defiant and cold, but not with us. "That, I know. We're all just a big, fucking happy family, aren't we, Dad? We. The Coles. The Followhills. The Rexroths. I mean, you and uncle Dean even dated Mom almost at the same time, didn't you? That's some modern shit right there. I guess I'm an old-school kind of guy. Sharing is not my jam."

My eyelid ticks with anger as I finally catch up with what my son is saying. I snap, "Language!" at the same time that Vicious corners Vaughn near the glass behind the staircase. He is not touching him, but he is still making sure our son knows he overstepped, and now he needs to listen to what we have to say. My head is reeling. I can't figure out where all of this is coming from. My son is a lot of things, but he is not prone to dramatics. Something happened.

Vicious chuckles, shaking his head before plastering his palm next to Vaughn's face and getting in his personal space. I feel the urge to break them apart, but I also know that Vaughn is the kind of kid that needs to be reminded what boundaries are. Vicious lifts a warning finger to Vaughn's face. "I love you. You're my son. It's in my blood to demolish anything that remotely endangers your wellbeing. But I will be clear on this, and only say it once—next time you talk about your mother like that, you and I are going to have a serious problem. A problem which will not limit itself to money, something I know you don't care about. I assure you that you will regret disrespecting her, or me, and just to set the record straight, Emilia never dated Dean and me at the same time. She dated Dean, and I was the asshole who tried to steal her away from him. Nod once if you understand this, twice if you still want me to confiscate anything that's not water or oxygen from your life for the next two months."

Vaughn nods once, his eyes narrowing into

slits as he scans his dad. My heart is in my throat. Vicious take a step back and irons Vaughn's tattered collar with his hand.

"Relationships are complex, son. So are people. What's bothering you?"

"Knight's existence is fucking bothering me."

I'm about to call him out on his language again, but then Vicious shoots me a not-now look. He has a point. I love my husband, but he cusses like a drunken sailor in an Irish bar. I promised myself I would not be a hypocritical parent before I had Vaughn, and so far, I have kept my promise.

I take a step toward them, placing a reassuring hand over my son's shoulder. I don't recall the exact moment when he stopped feeling soft under my touch, with chunky Pillsbury's baby arms and cheeks that seemed to have swallowed the rest of his features, to this young man, sinewy and resilient, all sharp edges and aristocratic features.

"What are you two up to now?" Vicious thrusts his chin toward our son. Knight and Vaughn grew up practically as brothers. They were born in the same month, for God's sake. But you couldn't find two people more different in personality and style. My child is cold, aloof, frivolous, and cruel at times, while Knight, like his dad, Dean, is open, candid, friendly, and was blessed with enough charm to enchant the entire nation with his cocky grin alone.

"It's not what he is doing; it's *who* he is doing."

"You're sixteen. You should not be doing anyone other than yourselves," Vicious quips. I laugh, and Vaughn rolls his eyes, something he is trying to refrain from doing, so I know he is really pissed.

"May I be ex-fucking-cused? And please, no more 'language' BS, Mom. We both know I learned it somewhere."

"Is this about Luna?" I probe, forever in Mama Bear mode.

Vaughn huffs out a laugh, shaking his head and swiveling toward the edge of the stairway again. "Yeah. Right. Like Luna would put out to Knight."

"Daria, then?"

I know my son has a secret he shares with Daria Followhill. Despite her being a senior and him a sophomore, there is a bond that connects them. But Daria is homecoming queen. Prom queen. Head cheerleader and the most popular girl in school. Coming at second place is not really an option for her, and so sometimes she tries to push Luna around, simply because she steals so much of the boys' attention without even trying.

But I also know my son's personality, and he is not easily affected by his gorgeous, senior friend. At first, I thought Vaughn and Daria were having sex, but when I confronted him about it, he just laughed and said, "I love you, Mom. I do. But if you really must know, I'd rather mess around with our neighbors' dog before I touch a bitch like Daria."

Did he get grounded for that kind of language? Yes.

Did he care? No.

"Asking me again and again will not make me open up, Dad. It will just make me want to punch more walls, and Ralph is already on my case." Ralph is our interior designer. He pops in every year or whenever Vaughn is having one of his angry phases. "The Devil Wears Walmart," he tells me every time he drops in for his usual let's-remodel-your-kitchen visit and sees my son. I don't think Vaughn is wearing Walmart, but I'm not quite sure what he *is* wearing. I just know he looks grunge and hard-edged, like his dad was, but in less a preppy way. I palm Vaughn's cheek, and he kisses the base of my palm before swatting my hand away.

"I just need to be alone for a few hours to get my shit together. Can I have that?" he asks.

"Of course." But what my mama didn't tell me is that we say of course, and we might even think it, when in reality, all we want to do is wrap our arms around our kids and take the pain away.

Later that night, I know Vaughn is out of the house because his car is not parked next to Vicious'. I slip into my shimmering pink nightgown, squirt hand cream on my hands and rub it nice and good all over my arms and neck. I walk over to the extra-large king-sized bed I share with Vicious. Our room is uniquely-designed, with dry-packed stone for walls and Egyptian cotton linen smoothed over a low, contemporary bed. Candle lights drop from the ceiling, and every wall is adorned with a different painting by me.

Painting one: A portrait of Vicious looking at an invisible camera.

Painting two: A portrait of me staring at a portrait of him with cherry blossoms in my hair.

Painting three: A glass frame containing all the notes we sent one another in high school. Before we found out we were in love with each other. When we simply hated how trapped we felt inside our own feelings.

Painting four: black canvas with drops of pink splashed onto it. Abstract. Wild. Intangible. Much like our feelings toward each another.

I notice the light pouring like a sunray from the slit under Vicious' office door and sigh. I turn off the lights and tuck myself into bed, staring up at the ceiling.

I read somewhere that once you become a mother, you stop being your own story's protagonist, and that changes the fabric of who you are, of how you perceive life. My son is far from perfect. He does, in fact, carry the same savagery of his father and a similar obsessive need to defy cultural expectations, like me. But I know deep down that his soul is gentle, just like his father's. Just like mine.

I drift off to sleep, knowing Vicious will stay awake until Vaughn is home, before I'm awakened by a weird sensation. Actually, weird may not be the right word for what I'm feeling. It is delightful, hot, and it makes my core tighten and quiver with desperate need.

Vicious' hot, wet tongue drags from the base of my sex up to my clit, where he halts, sucks it in with a groan, then bites softly before he releases it. I spread my legs wider on an instinct, a moan tumbling from my lips.

"Vaughn?" I ask in a haze, the fog of a building orgasm and sleep making me groggy and frantic at the same time. His hands dip and graze every curve of my body, and I writhe and arch underneath him, a willing subject to the king who owns my body.

"Still out. I called him earlier and he's on his way. We got ten minutes before the little devil comes back."

"And what are you planning to do in those ten minutes, Mr. Spencer?" I grin, dipping my fingers in his onyx-black hair, still thick and shiny. He looks up from between my legs and smirks, his lips wet and glossy with my need for him.

"Finish what we started this afternoon. On your

knees for me, Mrs. Spencer."

I'm about to stand up and do as I'm told when he pins me back to the bed with a light shove, flicking my clit with his thumb and using his other hand to prop my butt up.

"I think I'd like to torture you a little first."

"We don't have much time," I say, but my heart is not in it. I'm giggling like a schoolgirl.

Vicious gives me one last don't-mess-with-me look. "I'm not getting cockblocked by a sixteen-year-old emo kid, even if we share the same genetic code. Now, relax for me, Em."

He eats me up like I'm a French dessert, and my body is sizzling, blooming, coming alive, each sensitive nerve a red, shiny button he pushes. I'm shaking all over and my knees turn to jelly when he stops his licking, sucking, and tongue-thrusting abruptly, looming over me now, his arms boxing me just above my shoulders. He stares down at me, and all I can see in his eyes is the man I was born to love.

There was a lost boy who used to live there, too. And I love him just as much.

I think Vicious is going to say something, after depriving me of a forceful orgasm, but all he does is smash his lips against mine. Our teeth clash and I let out a drunken laugh while he fumbles with his black sweatpants, pushing them down and entering me missionary style. He hoists one of my legs over his shoulder and sinks into me all at once.

"Ohhh…" I moan. I can taste myself on my lips, a weird thing I've learned to like and even crave. He rides me slowly, pinning my hands up against our headboard and bringing his free hand down, dipping two fingers inside me, so that I'm deliciously stretched and begging for my release. He rides me with quiet intensity, taking his time, even though he knows that Vaughn will be here any minute. He likes to see me squirm and worry. Watch the anxiousness in my eyes. Even after all these years, it still turns him on, but the truth is, it turns *me* on, too.

"Hurry up," I groan.

"Sweetheart, don't forget who bosses whom around here." He goes even slower, and I'm panting, and wriggling, fighting him for more friction. I want to come. *I need to come.*

"Vaughn will be here any minute."

"He knows his parents have sex. Unless he still thinks we found him under a gooseberry bush."

I snort out a nervous laugh, and he takes my hands, which he pinned to the board, and plants them on his butt and back. "Shut up and let me fuck you, Emilia."

"Make me come, then," I order, my voice quivering. And it's a mistake, I know it before I'm even done uttering the words, because he pulls out halfway, his tip and some of his shaft still inside me, and begins to move in delicious circles, prolonging my orgasm even more. His fingers that were shoved inside my pussy a moment ago are now in my mouth. He is stuffing me with them so I won't be able to moan loudly.

"See? Problem solved. Now I can fuck you well into next week and our kid wouldn't even notice, because you won't make a sound."

Vicious has always been good and proper. He possesses the manners of the old-moneyed, but at the same time, he loves to watch me widen my eyes in horror with some of the things he says. Sometimes I do it just to get his rocks off. Then I remind him with a biting tongue that I'm not some damsel in distress.

The sound of the entry door opening and closing makes my eyes broaden. I stare at my husband with the horror of a woman who knows her son well enough to predict he will stop by our room to tell us goodnight so that we know he is here, because he knows we stay awake until he gets back home.

The smirk on Vicious' lips alone makes my core clench around him involuntarily, and he withdraws his fingers from between my lips, cups my mouth with his hand, and begins to ride me so hard and so fast, I'm worried he will tear me apart.

"Oh, Lord, oh, Lord, oh, Lord," I chant, my voice muffled by his palm. The spasm is violent, ripping at my insides like a tempest. It feels like an electric shock as he rides me into a place it will take me hours to recover from. The heat swirls in my stomach and the wetness pulling underneath us in bed. I tear my eyes away from Vicious', knowing that I could scream even through his hand if I see what's inside them, the tortured boy I fantasized about every night in my bed as a teenager. I come in his arms, wave after wave of pleasure slamming into me from within.

"Mom? Dad?" I hear Vaughn coming up the stairs, eating something crunchy. The click of a spoon against fine china. Cocoa Pops is my bet. The room reeks of sex and we are both sweating. The heady, sweet scent of my lust, combined with the saltiness of Vicious' cum dripping between us, is a dead giveaway to what we've been doing. And I shouldn't be embarrassed, but I am. Vicious rolls off of me and chuckles, covering his face with his forearm so that all I can see are his pearly-whites.

"Yes, honey," I yell back to Vaughn, clearing my throat when I realize how guilty and embarrassed I sound. "I'm just getting dressed for bed. Everything okay?"

"Can you stop by my room before you go to sleep?"

Vicious and I exchange looks. This is unlike Vaughn, but at least he passed by our door without knocking on it or pushing it open. Vicious gives me half a shrug, his eyebrows crinkling with amusement.

"I think we still have kiddie books in the attic if he needs a goodnight story."

I elbow his ribs lightly and roll my eyes. "I hate you."

"Your pussy didn't seem to get the memo." He moves over to his side of the bed and pushes his nightstand drawer open to produce a joint. I motion him with my hand to go outside to the patio, and he nods solemnly. I don't need Vaughn to see it and get any ideas. The women of the HotHole crew have successfully managed to shelter the kids from the fact that their fathers are perpetual stoners thus far. As far as my knowledge goes, none of them are smokers, thank God.

I pad barefoot to Vaughn's room down the hall in my fresh nightgown—a modest one at that—and knock before I open the door.

"Come in."

He sits on his bed, his back against the bedpost, worrying his lip and shooting a dart straight to the center of the board in front of his bed. He is wearing his usual outfit of a holey shirt—white, this time— and black skinny jeans that are at least two years old and have somehow become both tight and loose. Even I, as his mom, have to admit that he's got the rebellious edge down to an art. He dresses simply, but his look has character, personality, and flavor. Like a del Toro movie. You can recognize Vaughn without knowing that it's him, even from a few dozen yards.

I take a seat at the edge of his bed, cupping his bent knee. He focuses his gaze on me, a frown crossing his face.

"Where were you? It's two a.m.," I say. I can't really fault him for going out on a Friday night. He is a teenager, after all. But I sure as hell can fault him for coming back an hour later than he should have.

"Just a party." He shrugs.

"Daria's?" Daria Followhill throws a party every other weekend, something my sister, Rosie, and I give Mel—Daria's mother—a lot of crap about. Daria is notoriously snotty, something Jaime and Mel have a hard time coming to terms with. I honestly feel that at this point, my good friends have lost control of their daughter and their only expectation of her is to not fall pregnant or get addicted to meth before the school year ends. Daria is busier strategizing ruining other attractive girls' lives than college admissions. In fact, she made it clear to Mel and Jaime that college was not on her agenda.

"Yup," Vaughn says, popping the P with another unintentional eye roll.

"Who were you planning to see there?" It wasn't

Daria, that's for sure. And Daria would die before voluntarily inviting Luna anywhere. Daria grew up thinking Luna stole some of her precious limelight, especially since the boys have always been fond of her. So that is odd, considering Vaughn and Knight's crew take Luna with them everywhere.

Vaughn straightens his legs and leans forward, giving me rare eye contact. He licks his lips, which tells me that he is nervous, and that makes me nervous.

"Daria's in trouble."

"What kind of trouble?" I take a deep breath, bracing myself for the hit. Daria has always had her father's rebellious streak and determination. Combined with her mother's sarcasm and dancer genes, she quickly became an unstoppable force.

Prettiest.

Most talented.

And, therefore, *not* the nicest.

"I don't wanna rat her out, so you need to promise not to tell anyone. Not even Dad." He flings a warning finger toward me, and I take a second to think about it before offering him a silent nod. My heart beats faster. Vaughn is not a snitch. If he is coming to me with this, it means that he is worried, and Vaughn is never worried. He screams nonchalance. Well, actually, he utters it quietly, with a patronizing smirk.

"Words, Mom."

"I promise."

"Daria's having an affair."

I stare at him, dumbfounded, and blink a few times before a small smile expands on my face. "You mean, she has a boyfriend?"

My son stares at me like I'm a complete idiot. "No, Mom. Affair."

"Define affair."

"With Principal Prichard. That defined enough for you?"

My heart is lodged in my throat, and I am blinking away what must be tears. Daria just turned eighteen. Principal Prichard is not old, but he is almost my age. He *is* old for her. Thirty-six, to be exact.

She is a child.

I bathed her and cut her food into miniscule pieces, for Lord's sake.

I stay silent for the longest time, not entirely sure what to tell Vaughn.

"Thanks for the input. Anyway." He pokes me with his socked toes, groaning. "I'm covering for her scrawny ass as much as I can, but honestly, it's getting a little out of control and I don't need this bullshit, you know? We're about to start the second semester and I'm tired of watching for her shit and making up lies."

"Wait, how does it have anything to do with

Knight? You said he was the one you are mad at this afternoon."

"Oh." He scratches his chin, shrugging. "We flipped a coin. Knight lost. He was supposed to say something to his parents before shit hit the fan, but of course he bailed, because he is messing around with Cadence, Daria's best friend."

It's not what Knight is doing; it's who he is doing.

That makes sense now.

"How many people know about Daria and her affair?" I want to throw up at how twisted and ironic this whole thing is. Daria's parents had a forbidden teacher and student affair. She is well aware of that, and I wonder if it's her way to try to rile them up.

Vaughn shrugs. "Not many. Enough to get Daria all freaked out, but not enough to make her stop. He…" My son looks sideways, shaking his head on a sigh, like this is ridiculous, even to him. "Mom, he buys her crazy shit. I don't know how he affords that kind of crap on his salary."

"Language."

"Honestly, after everything I told you about how other kids are behaving, you should award me with a medal, not worry about my profanity."

"I can do both." I let loose a tired smile, but then I remember how complicated the situation is. I love Daria. I love her like a family member, and she is getting drawn into something very dangerous.

I look down at my hands. They're shaking.

I look up to my son. His eyes are searching mine.

Then I hear the words I shouldn't be hearing, from a person who shouldn't be in this room.

It's my husband, and he is standing at the door to Vaughn's room, one arm propped over the doorframe. "Drama in Todos Santos, who would have thought?"

I put my hand over Vaughn's, and he shoots a knowing glance at his dad.

"Guess you can call us *All Saints' Sinners*."

All Saints' Sinners is a YA spin-off series to the Sinners of Saint.
The first book in the series, Pretty Reckless, is due to come out early 2019.

Before you go:

Make sure you sign-up to my newsletter for one free e-book by me and a monthly free e-book by a bestselling author: eepurl.com/dgo6x5

Join my reading group, The Sassy Sparrows, for exclusive teasers, excerpts and giveaways: goo.gl/QZJ0NC

Facebook: www.facebook.com/authorljshen

Reading group: https://goo.gl/3eVXIq

Website: www.authorljshen.com

Instagram: www.instagram.com/authorljshen

More by L.J. Shen:

Tyed
Sparrow
Blood to Dust
Vicious (Sinners of Saint #1)
Defy (Sinners of Saint #0.5))
Ruckus (Sinners of Saint #2)
Scandalous (Sinners of Saint #3)
Midnight Blue

Coming soon: *Bane*
(Sinners of Saint Standalone Spinoff)

Before you go: check out the first chapter of my
latest novel,

Alex Winslow in another meltdown: arrested for DUI and possession of cocaine.

By Beth Stevenson, The Daily Gossip

British singer Alex Winslow was arrested again Tuesday night for driving under the influence and for possession of cocaine. The twenty-seven-year-old singer had been released from California's Lost Hill Sheriff's Station after a night in jail. A night during which, it is alleged, he swung on the bars of his cell and wrote the lyrics to his song "Wild Heaven" on the walls using a blue Sharpie given to him by a smitten station employee (a Sharpie he later used to sign her breasts).

As well as getting caught with three grams of cocaine in the glove compartment of his azure vintage Cadillac, the heartthrob is also accused of trying to seduce his way out of trouble when he got pulled over in the early hours on the Pacific Coast Highway cradling a nearly-empty bottle of whiskey.

The twelve-time Grammy winner allegedly unleashed his famous, one-hundred-million-dollar smile at the officer on the scene, a forty-three-year-old mother of three, saying, "You really are f***** arresting, love, but I reckon I'll be the one doing the cuffing tonight."

The "Man Meets Moon" singer infamously got arrested eight weeks ago for punching Steven Delton, owner of the website Simply Steven, and for stealing a Grammy statuette. Winslow stormed onto the stage at the Grammys mid-speech when fellow British singer William Bushell received the Best Album award, plucked the statue from Bushell's hand, lit a cigarette, and launched into a rant:

"Are you having a laugh? Raise your hands if you actually voted for this wanker without

getting bribed with a complimentary hand-job. Come on. Come. The. Fuck. On. His whole album sounds like background music at McDonald's. No offense. To McDonald's, not to Bushell. There wasn't even one creative track in the entire album. In fact, if creativity met this bloke in a dark alley, it would run the other way, screaming bloody murder. I'm taking this home. Doesn't feel too good when someone steals what's yours, eh, mate? Well, boo-fucking-hoo. It's called life, and it's a lesson you taught me."

Previously close friends and former London roommates, Bushell and Winslow had a falling out two years ago over model/socialite sensation, Fallon Lankford, and have been labeled enemies since. Both Brits slammed reports concerning bad blood between them. It has been alleged that Winslow's latest album, Cock My Suck—which peaked at number nine on Billboard and disappeared from the charts soon after, the worst in his career—had driven him into the arms of alcohol and cocaine.

Shortly after word got out of Winslow's arrest, Simply Steven ran an article titled, "Alex

Winslow: The End of an Era." It is believed that Mr. Delton is now looking to sue Winslow, after the latter assaulted him with a jab to the face when asked about Fallon Lankford's new love interest, Will Bushell.

Within hours of his second release, Winslow offered an apology through his long-time agent, Jenna Holden:

"Alex Winslow is deeply sorry for doing a number of things that were very wrong and for which he is ashamed. He would like to apologize to the officer who arrested him, stretching the apology to her husband, children, and the local church in which she volunteers. Winslow acknowledges his out-of-control behavior can no longer be overlooked, and for the sake of his loved ones, his fans, and himself, has decided to check himself into a rehabilitation facility in the state of Nevada. We kindly ask you to respect his privacy as he fights this very personal battle against his demons."

Winslow's former publicist, Benedict Cowen, who parted ways with the singer days after his Grammy meltdown, was not available for comment.

Comments (1,937)

xxLaurenxx
He is off-the-rails crazy. Also: off-the-rails hot.

Pixie_girl
Dude, McDonald's background music? Richhhh. Winslow's last album was so bad my ears bled for two weeks after listening to it.

Cody1984
#LeaveAlexAlone
(just kidding, he'll probably shove a finger into an outlet or something if we don't keep an eye on him.)

James2938
Guy's a sociopath. You can very clearly see it in his art.

BellaChikaYass
I echo that thought…but I'd still do him. ;)
xxLaurenxx
Me too! Lol
Pixie_girl
Sadly, me three.
James2938

Good, because he's not the kind
Of guy who can offer you more
than a quickie. He is bad news.
LITERALLY.

Chapter One

Indie

Six months later.

Tap. Tap. Tap, tap, tap, tap, tap.

The soles of my shoes slapped against the granite floor like a persistent canary. I had to dig my fingernails into my thighs to make my legs stop bouncing to the rhythm of my restless, foolish heart.

Shut up, heart.

Chill out, heart.

Stop fussing, heart.

There was no need to panic. Not even a little. Not even at all.

I was going to get the job.

I elevated my head, flashing the woman sitting across from me my biggest, most enthusiastic smile.

"When we advertised the job for a PA position, we kind of, sort of, what's the word I'm looking for...? *Lied.*" Slamming her chrome MacBook shut, she splayed her bony, manicured fingers on top of it, showcasing a ring that must've cost enough to buy the better half of my up-and-coming neighborhood.

My throat bobbed, and I smoothed down my tattered pencil skirt. Actually, it wasn't even mine. It was Natasha's, my brother's wife, and two sizes too large at the waist. I only ever got called back from food chain restaurants that didn't require a suit, so I'd had to improvise. I tucked my knotted ankles under my chair, sparing my interviewer my silver Oxford shoes, a hint of my personality I'd forgotten to disguise.

Everything in the woman's office screamed excess. Her desk, white and sleek; the seats made of alabaster leather; and the bronze chandelier dripping down between us like liquid gold. The Hollywood Sign poured from her floor-to-ceiling window in all its promising, beautiful, broken promises glory. So close you could see the dirt clinging to the white letters. Her workplace was the size of a ballroom. There wasn't a drop of color or personality in this office, and not by accident.

Jenna Holden. Powerhouse agent to the biggest Hollywood stars. Owner of JHE Group. She didn't have time to get personal. Least of all with the likes of me.

"You're not looking for a PA?" The forced smile

on my face crumbled. I needed this job like Mark Wahlberg needed to show his real junk in *Boogie Nights*. Really, *really* bad. Case in point: I was living with my brother, his wife, and kid, and as much as they loved me, I'm sure they loved not having to share their one-bedroom apartment with a twenty-one-year-old avant-garde slob slightly more. My only source of transportation was my bicycle, which in L.A. was the equivalent of getting from A to Z on a dead turtle's back.

"I'm looking for…*something*." Jenna tipped her chin down, bowing a thinly plucked eyebrow. "And it does involve some assisting."

My patience was hanging by a thread, ready to jump ship. I was hungry, thirsty, and desperate for the job. *Any job*. Summer had kicked my ass, and all the blue-collar positions had been filled by acne-ridden teenagers. This was the third time I'd come into JHE for this vague job this month. First, I'd gone through the HR girl who'd left me waiting for forty minutes because her pedicure appointment ran late. Then, Jenna's personal assistant had grilled me like I was fresh back from an ISIS training camp. Finally, I'd met with the mega agent herself, and now she was telling me I'd been misled this whole time?

"Tell me, Indigo, how carefully did you read the job description?" She sat back in her chair and laced her fingers together. She wore a crisp, buttoned shirt tucked into black velvet pants, and a smug smile. Her champagne-blonde hair was pulled into a painful looking bun, and my skull burned just from looking at the way her skin pulled around her hairline.

"Careful enough to repeat it by heart."

"Is that so? In that case, please do."

My nostrils flared. I decided to humor her one last time before collecting my bag and remainder of self-esteem and walking away.

*"PA needed: resilient, responsible, patient, and thick-skinned. Non-drinker, **NO DRUGS**, with a flair for arts and life. If you're twirling on the sidelines of mainstream, have great attention for detail, and don't mind long hours and endless nights, we're looking for you. *NDA needed, criminal record will be checked."*

I pushed a copy of my job application, tapping it with my finger. "This is me. Sans the twirling part. I'm prone to migraines. Now, can you tell me why I'm here?"

"What I'm looking for is a savior. A nanny. A friend. You're the closest thing to perfect I've found, but frankly, this whole thing is going to be a lot like an organ transplant. We won't know if you're a match until we put you two together."

I blinked, studying her like she was a mythological creature. If this was a joke, I'd officially lost my sense of humor.

She stood up and began to pace, her arms folded behind her back. "I have a client. No, not a client. *The* client. One of the hottest names in the industry this decade. He got himself into hot water recently and now he needs a big bucket of ice to cool his name off. Drugs, women, ego the size of China—you name it, he's suffering from it. Your job is not to book flights and make coffee. He's got an arsenal of people doing that for him. But you will be there when he goes on tour. You'll cater to his emotional needs. You'll make sure he doesn't snort cocaine backstage, or stay out late, or miss a show. You'll be there to grab his hand and pull him away when he gets into an argument with a journalist or a paparazzo. Your job, in short, is to keep him healthy and alive for three months. Think you're up for the challenge?"

Her words were so sincere and sharp, they sank into my skin like teeth.

A savior. A nanny. A friend.

"That's…a lot of responsibility. Sounds like that someone is in big trouble."

"Trouble is his middle name, a part of his charm, and the reason why I have a Xanax tab in my purse at all times." She cracked a bitter smile.

TMI, TMI, TMI.

"If he's in no shape to go on tour, why is he doing it?"

155

"He was supposed to leave six months ago and canceled for personal reasons. If he cancels again, he'll have to pay thirty million dollars to the production companies. The insurance will never pay up, considering the cause of termination was him swimming in enough cocaine to bake a five-tier wedding cake."

I tapped my toes against the shiny floor some more, gnawing at my lower lip. Jenna stopped moving around. She was now standing in front of me, her thin, golden Prada belt twinkling like a sad eclipse.

"Three months on the road. Private jet. Best hotels in the world. If you've somehow managed to hang onto the leftovers of your innocence in this city and want to keep it, I'd advise against taking the job. But if you have a thick skin and a taste for adventure, know this—this job will change your bank account, your path, and your life."

She sounded serious. Concerned. Every word had a weight and it sat heavy on my chest. "You'll sign a non-disclosure agreement. You'll take what you see to your grave. And you'll get paid mad bank."

Mad bank? Who talked like that? L.A. showbiz people. That's who.

"Mad bank?" I asked.

"A hundred thousand dollars for every month of

your employment."

Beat.

Beat.

Beat.

Three beats had passed before I sucked in air, remembering I needed to breathe.

Somewhere in the distance, I heard office folk snort-laughing next to the vending machine. A printer spitting out papers. A spoon clinking in a mug. My gnawing intensified, as it did when my nerves got the best of me, and the metallic taste of blood spread inside my mouth.

Three hundred thousand dollars.

Three months.

All my financial problems—gone.

"Who is he?" I looked up, my voice cracking like an egg. Did it matter? Not really. At this point, he could be Lucifer himself, and I'd still accompany him on a lengthy tour in hell. Natasha and Craig's bills were piling up. Ziggy needed tubes in his ears—every winter my nephew cried and screamed himself to sleep. We had to tie socks around his little fists to keep him from clawing at his ears until they bled. We couldn't even afford a new bed for him, and his chubby legs constantly got stuck between the bars of his cradle. This offer was a no-brainer. The only issue would be parting ways with my family, but even that came with a big chunk of relief.

My brother wasn't the best person to hang out with right now.

Besides, I'd been babysitting two-year-old Ziggy since the day he was born. This person was supposedly a grown-ass man. How hard could it be?

"It's Alex Winslow," Jenna supplied.

Evidently, the answer to my question is 'next to impossible.'

Winslow was huge. His songs were shoved down your throat by every radio station like he was the only person on the continent with vocal cords. But what truly worried me was that he seemed unapologetically arrogant. Alex Winslow looked through people like it was an Olympic sport and he wanted to make the queen proud, which was just one of the reasons why he'd managed to create beef with every person with a pulse in Hollywood. That was common knowledge, even if you tried to avoid gossip like the plague, which I did. Wherever he went, a string of reporters and palpitating fangirls followed. I'd get heat the minute his fans spotted me. The paparazzi shadowed him everywhere but to the bathroom. I once read in a gossip magazine—dentist appointment—that some girl had to shut down her Instagram account after partying with Winslow because a dark net website put a bounty on her head. Twenty grand was collected to predict her death date—*"fulfilling your prediction is entirely optional,"* they said.

Last but not least, Winslow was the most antiauthority mainstreamist in Hollywood. Not too long ago, he was arrested for DUI, and I hated, despised, *loathed* drugs and alcohol. Which basically meant that our "organ transplant," as Jenna had referred to it, would likely result in two casualties and one epic failure.

I cradled my face in my hands, letting out a breath.

"This is the part where you say something." Jenna's cherry red lips twitched.

I cleared my throat and straightened my posture.

Time to put on your big girl panties and make sure they stay dry for three months, despite him looking like Sean O'Pry's hottest brother.

"I promise to keep him safe and sound, Ms. Holden."

"Good. Oh, and I'm going to say this once to keep my conscience clear: don't fall in love with the guy. He's not the white picket fence type." Jenna waved a hand and scrolled her phone, pressing her thumb onto it and making a call.

"I'll try my best." My jaw muscles twitched as I swallowed a sneer. Alex Winslow was beautiful in a way storms were—only from afar. Just like them, he had the power to sweep and ruin you, two things I was too busy surviving to entertain.

"If your best is good enough, then you should

survive this. I'll have my assistant print out the paperwork. Any questions?" She fired some instructions on the other line to said assistant, then ambled toward the door.

"When are we leaving for his tour?" I peeked over my shoulder, my fingernails burrowing into the armrest.

"Wednesday."

"That's two days away."

"Good at math." She sneered. "That's an unexpected plus. I'll get the paperwork. The tour is called 'Letters from the Dead' and is supposed to revive his career. Be right back."

I remembered that song. It was the soundtrack to my senior year, when everything looked so final and wrong.

Love is just a fraud,
Excuse me for being goddamn bold,
You asked me to believe,
As if I had some fucks to give.

With the door closing behind her, I sat back and blew a lock of blue hair away from my face. Crazy laughter bubbled in my throat, eager to pour out.

I was going to make three hundred thousand dollars and hang out with the biggest rock star in the world for three months. I looked up, and the chandelier winked at me mischievously.

I thought it was a sign.

Made in the USA
Middletown, DE
21 November 2018